(Prolefeed)

"I... want to live so as to satisfy my whole capacity for living, and not so as to satisfy just my reasoning capacity alone... what does reason know? Reason knows only what it has managed to learn."

--Fyodor Dostoevsky

FANTASTIQUE UNFETTERED

A PERIODICAL OF LIBERATED LITERATURE

#3 Summer/Fall 2011

FANTASTIQUE UNFETTERED

Issue Three (Prolefeed) ISBN: 978-0-9831709-4-5
An M-Brane Press Publication
Publisher: Christopher Fletcher

Fiction Editor, Layout, Incidental Art: Brandon H. Bell | Poetry Editor, Associate Editor: Alexandra Seidel |Art & Design Consultant: M. S. Corley | Slush, Editorial Assts.: William Wood, Jaym Gates | Contributing Artists: E.M. Jensen, Kirsty Greenwood, Luis Beltran

Fantastique Unfettered is published by M-Brane Press. Send submissions to editors@fantastiqueunfettered.com. Find guidelines on the website: www.fantastique-unfettered.com

Suggested Retail Price: 9.99. Actual prices may vary. Order via Amazon, Barnes & Noble, and more.
Newstand distribution through Ingram, Baker & Talor, and more.

Reclamation...

I'm researching an editorial for our fourth issue, an attempt to offer a non-theistic, optimistic response to Thomas Ligotti's *The Conspiracy Against the Human Race*. Which is an odd thing to type since I'd prefer not to apply labels like optimistic or pessimistic to myself.

His book poses a simple question: Is life worth living? But he gets the answer wrong. While I am sure of this, it is eye-opening to explore why we believe as we do, and more importantly, what we know to be true.

The issue of Fantastique Unfettered you are about to read is subtitled (Prolefeed.) In considering what this means to me, and the oppressive, pessimistic visions of George Orwell, I find two snippets of his words echoing in my brain... *Under the spreading chestnut tree/ I found you and you found me...* and of course his prediction that the future of humanity is a face crushed beneath a booted foot.

It is enough to convince one to throw in with Ligotti and his lot, and call for a mass 'calling it quits.'

And yet, Orwell wasn't writing about some blood-slick and distant future world, but his present world, in flux. We are again in flux, in a time of --from ground level... sometimes from beneath booted-foot level-- increased change. And many of us worry where that change takes us.

An SF grand master suggested that civil servant equals civil master. We know not to trust The Man, but have pigeon-holed Him into one identity: representative of The State. But the guise as often takes the form of a smiling CEO, the truth-defining mouthpieces of a smattering of jealous gods, or the voices on our radio airwaves. The strong and the righteous shall abide no dissenting views: they will let us know what to think and know to be true.

Prolefeed should be drivel for the masses. Porn and pulp.

What we offer instead is prose and poetry from 'ground level.' Here is what our world looks like. You may see it more clearly for all the time spent on The Way or within a nightmare of spiders and human weakness. We don't do didactic. And still... even a short story or verse might hold lessons about carrying on in this world.

Prolefeed is an act of reclamation. It is the dissenting views, expressed and set free for all who would hear. It is, as well, a denial of those who see the facts of suffering and declare ours a hopeless case.

Is life worth living? You bet. But it's rough. We ask your trust, for a bit. We've some dreams to share with you. Let's go...

--Brandon H. Bell August, 21st, 2011

And Discovery

Poets bring us voices out of a darkness that we did not understand nor were even aware of before. They are mediums, give shape to things unknown, unfelt, give words to unvoiced thoughts within and without. This is their gift, their words for us, to hold, to swallow, or to speak out loud.

The unknown darkness--loneliness, longing, hurt, and love--are the playground of dream and daydream, sometimes of nightmares. They create within us half formed thoughts that are made whole when a page is turned or a cover closed, such is the magic that writers wield. Readers may not understand how it works, and they don't need to. The how has no part in that state of wonder.

For me, what makes a poem unique is not first and foremost the poem itself, but its echo, its shadow, the way I can walk down a street half dreaming and suddenly hear it in my head "I need to stub my soul on yours[.]" That poetry is the sort of thing that starts out as a single note and ends in an avalanche. And then, when you realize that running away from that avalanche is pointless, all you can do is stop and listen. After, the world is not as it was before. And what would that be if not magic?

Stop running and *listen.*

FU #3 (Prolefeed): Enjoy.

--Alexandra Seidel, August 11th,2011

Contents

Issue Three| Summer/Fall 2011

NonFiction

Poetry

Fiction

Relative Weights and Measures
by
Bruce Boston

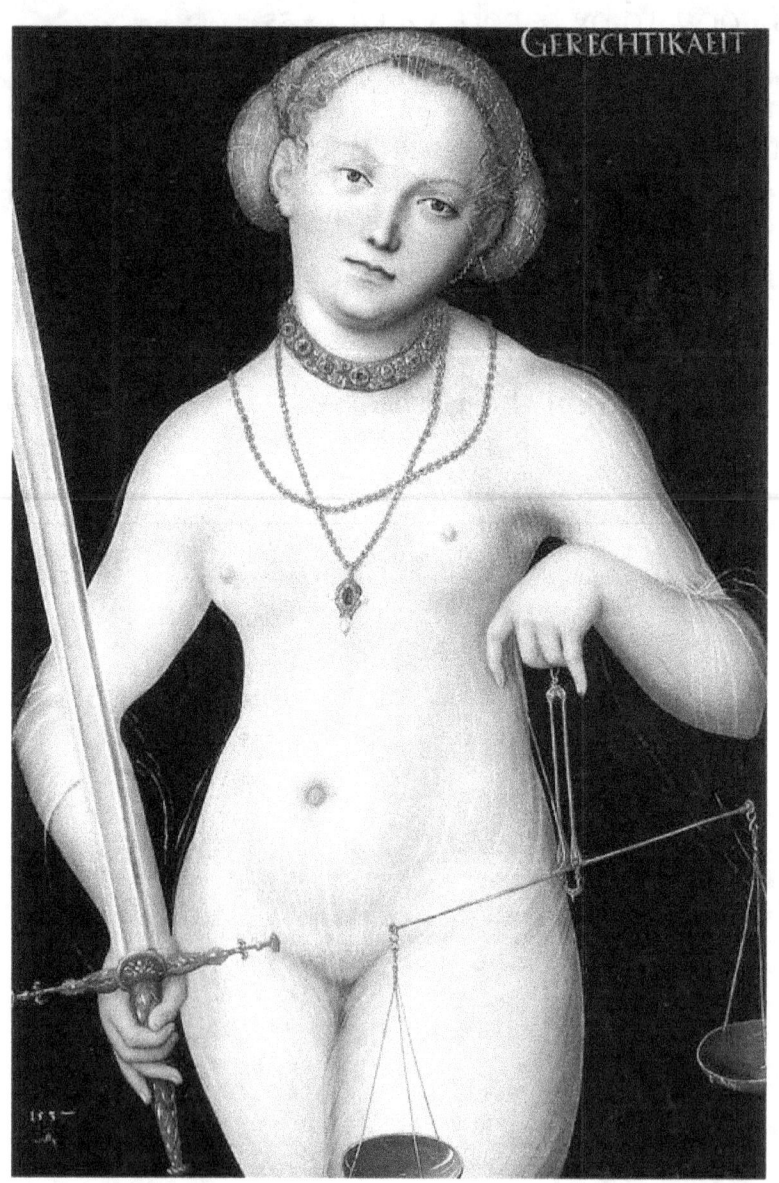

I'll trade you
a hundred pounds of feathers
for a pound of gold.

When I apply the yardstick
to the racing Bugatti
its wheelbase is shorter.

A quart and a half
of nepenthe drowns
seven drams of sorrow.

My unconscious mind
proves too large
for the ten gallon hat.

I'll trade you
three hundred pounds of butter
for a rack of AK-47s.

Whenever her hair
grows longer than her waist
she reaches for the scissors.

First Born

by

Samantha Kymmell-Harvey

Her first memory was of a bright brass doorknob. She grasped it and her fingers stuck together like a fist. She released it, leaving little crimson fingerprints behind. They were the only proof of her existence. She was no ghost, but a flesh and blood girl the harmonious discord of her mother's tenderness and her father's cruelty. A pair of pale hands scooped her up from the moist floor and the door creaked open.

Her second memory was a lullaby. A sweet voice sang to her while her feet soaked in a basin, raw from scrubbing. Yet still the dried blood snaking between her toes would not wash away. Those stains were her tattoo; her birthmark. That gentle voice whispered in her ear, "Beware of the man with the blue beard, my first born. Though he is your father, he will not spare you. But I will protect you for as long as I still breathe."

14

Those words etched themselves deeply into her young heart. She learned to walk soundlessly, passing from room to room undetected. On those muted toes, she pinched stale bread from the kitchen and drained forgotten cups of tea. She learned to hold her tongue except when she knew she was alone. Trusting in the shadows, she mastered the art of invisibility.

But loneliness does not come naturally to children and First Born was no exception. She had no one with whom to play hide and seek in the hall of armor. As a one person game, she simply called it "hide" and she never lost. Sometimes, when she found new places to conceal herself, she'd hear her father's heavy footsteps pass by. Holding her breath, she'd imagine him finding her, taking her in his arms, and hugging her into his blue beard. But he

"Beware of the man with the blue beard." First Born whispered into her ear, "Though he is your husband, he will not spare you. But I will be your friend for as long as I still breathe."

was not that kind of father and she reminded herself to breathe again.

She often heard his raspy voice and smelled his pipe smoke stale in the curtains. Once she found a muddy boot print in the foyer. Standing naked sole to caked sole, her two feet fit snugly inside the soggy earth print. Would she grow to be her father's size? Was she like him? Or did she take after her mother? Not daring to abandon the shadows, those little stolen pleasures sated her curiosity.

The day First Born lost the gentle voice she was tangled in the branches of the old apple tree beside the iron gate humming her lullaby. The notes stuck to her tongue like molasses and she'd start over, singing the melody with intense concentration. But the spring breeze carried a voice up from the gutter. Her voice, pleading and quaking. Her shriek pierced the silence on that sunless afternoon. First Born lowered herself and peered into the gutter. At the end of the pipe, deep in the castle's depths, two pale blue eyes looked back, unblinking. She never heard her lullaby again.

Those heavy boots trod up from the basement and down the corridor into the study. The blue-bearded man screamed, smashing a vase into shards and shiny powder. He threw his golden mirror from the window into the lake and he kicked off his boots, denting the wooden panels. First Born watched him from the keyhole, pleased that his bloodstained feet matched her own.

When the moon flooded the garden silver, First Born heard his cries. Creeping into the tree above her weeping father, she rustled neither leaf nor fruit.

"Why do you cry, noble sir?" Her light voice carried on the night breeze.

"Because I have lost my love and I am lonely," he said.

"I too am lonely. Will you be my friend?"

"The moon and mortal man cannot be friends." He reached towards the pale orb, "But please, send me another love."

First Born did not reply. With great patience, she listened as the sobbing subsided into the shallow gasps of slumber.

Blue Beard returned from town the next morning with a young blonde beauty upon his steed. First Born followed them from room to room, soaking in every detail her father imparted to his new bride. She smelled of lavender and lemons -- a country noble's daughter. The New Bride smiled a horse's smile upon discovering her wardrobe full of exquisite gowns. The blue-bearded man grinned, knowing she was satisfied.

That first night, the new wife slept alone.

"Beware of the man with the blue beard." First Born whispered into her ear, "Though he is your husband, he will not spare you. But I will be your friend for as long as I still breathe." And she slid under the covers, warming her feet on the woman's exposed legs.

"There is a little ghost with icicles for feet," she complained at breakfast.

Blue Beard laughed, revealing his crooked yellow teeth, "You are too old to believe in ghosts, my love."

The New Bride nodded, not wanting to upset her husband, but that night, she decided to lock her door to keep the spirit away.

First Born sat underneath her father's desk softly singing her lullaby. The clock struck two. Not a soul stirred in the darkness, except the little ghost. She couldn't sleep. Her dreams had turned to nightmares of her mother's death. She missed that gentle voice, missed being cradled in her arms. 'Why not play with the New Bride?' she thought, 'she believes in ghosts after all.' But when she found the woman's door would not open, First Born passed the rest of the night plotting her revenge.

"How did you sleep?" The Blue Bearded man asked the next morning.

"Much better. The little ghost with the icicle feet must not have been haunting last night."

When the couple departed on their hunting trip, First Born returned to the New Bride's bedchamber. She opened the wardrobe and took a pair of white lace gloves from the drawer. They smelled like the country. She pulled them over her own bony fingers. She thought she looked like a lady. But something else drew her attention --the New Bride's favorite gown: a moss green confection from Paris. It was love at first sight. First Born slid it over her skeletal frame and twirled in front of the mirror. "I am the daughter of the noble Blue Beard," she said, running a hand through her long, dirty hair, "You must envy my beauty."

Upon discovering her missing gown and gloves, the young wife ran to her husband, "That little ghost has gotten into my finery!"

"Nonsense, what does a ghost need clothes for?"

"You have taken them from me then. Since you have no servants in the house, who else is there to blame?"

Blue Beard stuffed his gnarled hands into his pocket and produced a shiny brass key ring containing three keys: a large, a medium, and a small. Handing them to his wife he said, "You may search every room in this castle. It will prove my innocence, but you must promise me one thing."

"Yes?" the woman asked, excited at

16

the thought of discovering more riches.

"The smallest key unlocks the chamber below the grand stairs. You must swear to me that you will never enter it."

"But you said . . ."

"Swear it!"

The blonde beauty hesitated for a moment, but in the end, she agreed as she always did, "I promise, my love."

First Born followed the sound of the bride's impish giggling. The New Bride discovered yet another room full of gowns and hats and gloves. She emerged from the Blue Room, neck weighed down by the strands of pearls, hair stuffed into an ostrich plumed hat. First Born stood in front of her, but the New Bride did not see her. Her eyes were full of jewels.

Another lock clicked open and the door moaned to the greedy little bride. It revealed the most luxurious ballroom in all of Europe. Its golden chandelier was crafted by the dwarves in the mountains of Norway. Its marble floor was quarried by the giants who dwelled in the hills of Rome. Its brocade draperies were sewn by the nimble hands of the French fairies. And its mirrors glittered in frames of unicorn horn. Clapping her hands together, she waltzed onto the dance floor. With each pirouette, she admired herself in the mirror. She saw a pale face, dark hair hanging in ropes over dark eyes. Not her

face. Not her eyes. But when she blinked, it was gone.

The little key felt hot in her palm. She knew her missing items had been hidden in the forbidden chamber. Blue Beard was only testing her intelligence. He would not outwit her. None of his riches could replace her French dress. She locked up the ballroom and hurried down the corridor, jewels tinkling like bells. And when she reached the plain wooden door under the grand stairs, she inserted the key and twisted.

First Born smelled tobacco in the air. Her father was near. She retreated into the arms of the shadows. The door slammed shut and there was a scream. Three round pearls rolled like marbles from under the door and came to rest at the girl's bloody toes.

That night, the little ghost came to warm her feet, but found the bed empty. She opened the wardrobe, finding it empty too. First Born sought comfort in the old apple tree by the iron gate, singing her lullaby with her untrained tongue. And the night wind smelled of sweet lavender and of sour decay.

For six years, Blue Beard begged the moon to send him a true love, the only cure he knew for loneliness. And she saw fit to send him a bride, each more beautiful than the last, each greedier than the last. But the moon never sent a playmate. So the little ghost survived in the shadows of the dusty castle, collecting pearls, fans, and gowns as tokens of her lost friends. In the black of the night, she haunted the new brides, "Beware of the man with the blue beard. Though he is your husband, he will not spare you. But I will be your friend for as long as I still breathe."

The seventh year brought a winter bride to the castle. She arrived with the sunset upon a rain-gray stallion. The woman asked to stay the night, and after they supped together, the blue-bearded man was smitten. He asked her to be his wife. She smiled with her dark violet lips, her unnaturally blue eyes gleaming. He couldn't see she was nothing like the others. She was made of sharp bones, her face a taut pale drum with a nose like a vulture. She never took tea or water. She hardly ate. Worst of all, the woman smelled of rotting flesh -- the daughter of a tanner, or maybe a butcher.

The first night, as the Winter Bride slumbered, she did not hear the pitter patter of frozen little toes. First Born marveled at her skeletal features deepened by the light of the full moon. Her pulse quickened as she whispered, "Beware of the man with the blue beard. Though he is your husband, he will not spare you. But I will be your friend for as long as I still breathe."

The Winter Bride moaned as if awake, yet her eyes did not open. Rolling onto

her side, she spoke, "Beware of the little ghost who thinks no one can see her. Her loneliness will be her undoing."

Frightened, the girl retreated into the darkness, but the Winter Bride slept serenely until morning.

"I heard a voice last night," the strange woman said as they strolled arm in arm through the snow-drenched garden.

"It was just the wind, my love." Blue Beard kissed her on the cheek. "Or merely a dream."

"I think there is a ghost," she said, touching an evergreen bough with the tip of her sharp white fingernail. The bough bleached and rotted, showering needles onto the frozen ground. The blue bearded man did not notice, for he was too captivated by his wife's sapphire eyes. But First Born noticed from the safety of the apple branches. Looking down, she saw those wicked eyes. And those wicked eyes saw her too.

At lunch, the woman left a chicken breast on a plate in the kitchen. At supper, she left a bowl of stew.

"You're trying to make friends with the rats, I see." Blue Beard said.

"No, it's the ghost I'm after."

But First Born was not in the kitchen. Nor was she close enough to smell the garlicky broth. Instead, the little ghost lay on an empty shelf in the library mending the holes in her invisibility.

Humming her lullaby, she played with the three silvery pearls. They felt smooth rolling in her palm, chilling her fingers. She wondered what the Winter Bride would bleed when lured into the chamber beneath the stairs.

The dawning sun stained the palace walls scarlet. First Born awoke and listened. Silence. She left the library and took the hidden passageway to the kitchen. The soup still remained untouched, though the bread had been nibbled. Her stomach gurgled. Like a wild animal, she poured the soup down her throat and gnawed the bread in hunks so large they nearly gagged her. Brushing the crumbs from her soiled chemise onto the floor, heavy footsteps above startled her.

First Born returned to her corner in the library. She gasped when she saw the pearls were gone. And the fan. And the Parisian gown. Her first cry seared her throat like a knife. Tendrils of death's aroma turned her stomach sour and she retched. The Winter Bride had robbed her.

"Why have you withheld such fineries from me, dear husband?" the woman twirled around the study holding the moss green gown over her plain black dress.

"I hide nothing from you, my love," he said.

But First Born could not take her eyes off the woman, feeling jealousy's dagger in her lonely heart. A voice from deep within her memory told her to be patient, to be calm.

"I don't believe you. In this impressive palace, surely I have not seen every treasure you possess," the Winter Bride said.

Blue Beard sighed and dipped his quill into the ink well. "What do you want of my things? You posses your own exotic treasures."

"But they are not enough."

First Born watched in delight as her father handed the Winter Bride his keys.

"My home is your home," he said, "you may go anywhere you please. Except for one room. The smallest key unlocks the chamber beneath the grand stairs. If you love me, you will not go there."

"I swear it, my sweet."

The blue-bearded man collapsed in his desk chair, shoulders shaking. He gripped the jar of ink in his hand. Throwing his head back, he gave a great shout, shattering the silence. It shattered the jar too, black liquid smothering the red between his calloused fingers.

The rusting hinges of the door sang their warning as the Winter Bride entered the forbidden chamber. First Born crept in behind her, holding her breath to keep from retching again. Despite the puddles of blood, the Winter

Bride did not scream. She stepped over the corpses, whose empty socket stares begged her to flee. But it was too late. The heavy boots descended the steps.

"Alas, you have disobeyed me and now you shall join them," Blue Beard said, his sword ready.

The Winter Bride only laughed. She turned around, revealing her true face; a naked skull, black eyes ablaze. "No, it is you who will die, my dear husband," she said, her hand wielding a scythe. She cut Blue Beard down easy as wheat.

Lady Death held her bony hand out to First Born who crouched behind the door. "Come with me, and you will never be lonely. Though I am Death, I will be your friend for as long as you still breathe."

Author's Note:

In Welsh legend, Blodeuedd (blod-EH-yeth) was the wife of the hero Lleu Llaw Gyffes (THLAY THLOU GUH-fes), made quite literally for him. The story begins with Lleu's mother, Arianrhod (ah-ree-AN-rod), who was to be the foot holder of her uncle Math but only if she was a virgin. Math asked her to step over a magic wand to prove her virginity, and as she did so she gave birth to two sons, Dylan (who rushed to the sea almost immediately) and his brother. Because Arianrhod was ashamed, she refused to acknowledge her second son, saying to Gwydion (GWID-ee-yon), her brother, first that her son would have no name except from her and then that he would have no arms except from her. With his skillful art of illusion and crafty lies, Gwydion managed to trick Arianrhod into naming her son Lleu Llaw Gyffes and arming him. But her last curse ~ that Lleu would have no wife of a race on the earth ~ Gwydion could not fool his sister into appeasing. Instead, he went to Math, and the two wizards fashioned the maiden Blodeuedd from the flowers of oak, broom, and meadowsweet to be Lleu's bride. But matters of the heart are never simple, and, once when Lleu was away, Blodeuedd met Gronw Bebyr (GROHN-oo Pebr) and loved him at first sight with her entire floral being and he her. The two conspired to kill Lleu so that they might be together, but killing Lleu involved a set of complicated circumstances, which Blodeuedd enticed out of her husband. When Lleu was in his vulnerable state, Gronw slew him with a poisoned spear. Lleu, however, did not die but became an eagle. When Gwydion finally found his nephew, he restored Lleu and they took a terrible revenge on the lovers, Lleu killing Gronw and Gwydion transforming Blodeuedd into an owl.

23

Blodeuedd, or, The Maiden of Flowers
by
Robert E. Stutts

Here is what I remember:

Drowsy mornings in spring, the hum in the air as the bees rose
hungry for nectar and the gentle extension of tongues,
a probing sting, ceaseless and delicious.

The breath of the sky upon the earth, sweeping this way
and that, whispering pollen-heavy secrets, small gossips from
cloud-ringed mountains or sly asides from salty marshes.

Sleeping sheathed in snow or ice, the memory of spring buried
deep in the earth, but the pulse of expectation shuddering slightly,
the slowed heartbeat curving and craving petals and leaves.

Here is what I remember:

The unfolding of blossoms in the frost-lined light of morning,
waking beneath the hands of your great-uncle and your uncle-
father, their arrogant, proud fingers shearing, shifting, shaping.

The delicate stitcheries of oak flowers limned into human limbs,
the yellow vulva of broom orchestrated into cradle and cauldron, forge and bellows,
all of me then slippered into clusters of meadowsweet smoothed and stretched full.

Gone were the bees and their kisses, no more the long gilding flights of pollen.
My first words were your name, shining links of chain dropped from my lips.
The only way to love you was to keep a dream of your death in my heart.

24

Here is what I know:

Instead of leaves I wove arms and legs, rooted no more, nothing to connect me to my mother
but the soles of those clumsy feet, my toes alight in grass and dirt, air on fire in my lungs.
I was made in flowers to have a master, but I wanted another, who smelled of honey and limes.

We did murder you, we wore your blood in our hair and on our brows. I did not forget your
    uncle,
that he would coax you from your eagle-skin, that punishment would follow. But
for a time I was free to dance among the floating bees as if they might kiss me again.

The owl sings at night, flower-ringed eyes all that recall that flower-faced maiden you wed.
I am never far from your window now, though my lonely song is not a call for you
but for the lost warmth of the sun on my face and the dream of the world spinning around me.

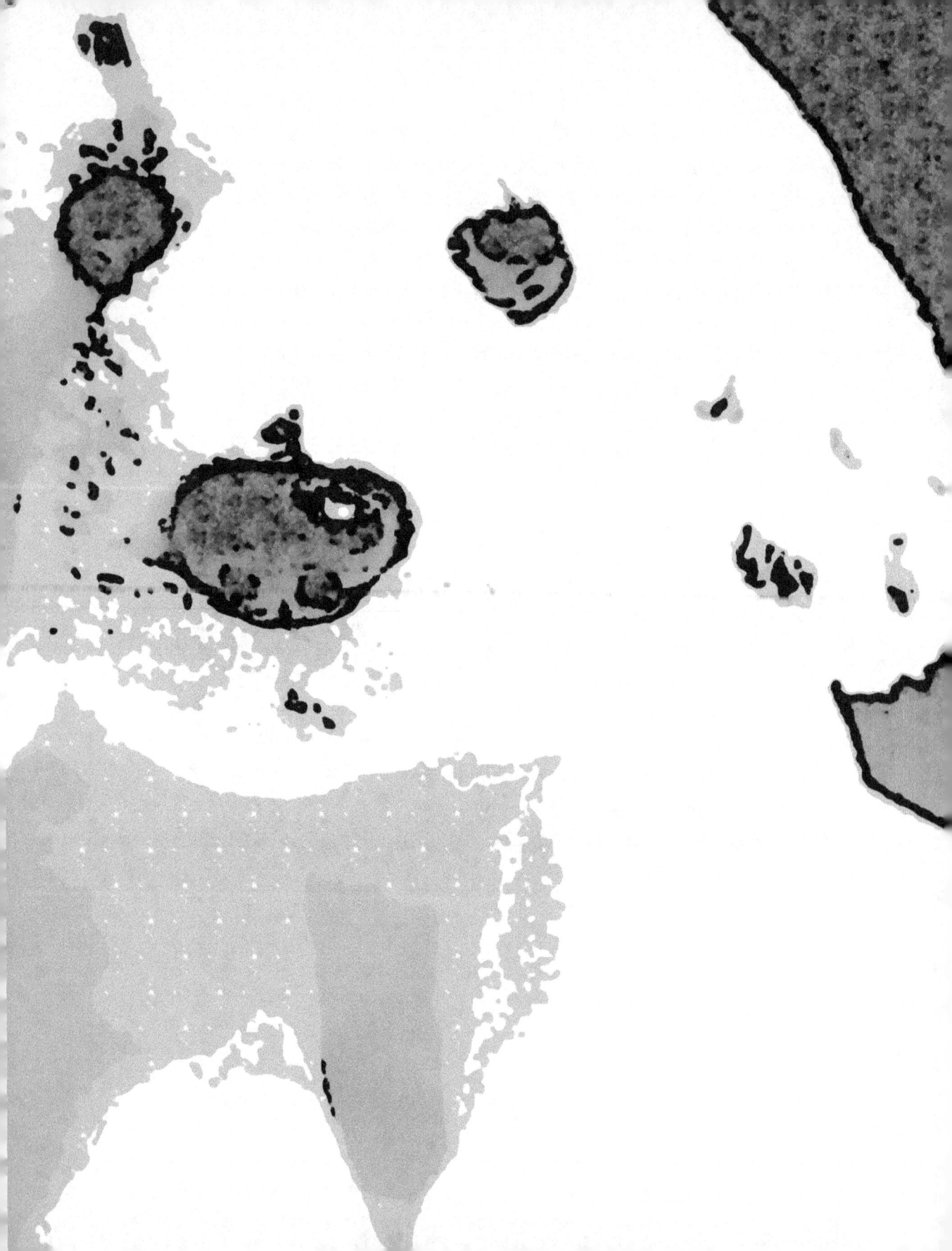

The Singularity
of Puppies

by
Michael Furlong

This story is dedicated to the real Fredric Brown
(1906-1972).

"There's so much I need to tell you before the world ends," Fredrick the puppy said. The puppy wagged his tail like a rattlesnake striking. "So so much. Where do I start?" Panting.

"Start at the beginning," said Joey Brown, the puppy's owner.

"There's a monster living under the next door neighbor's house."

"Mrs. Bass's house?"

"It's my mother."

"Where I found you?"

"Yes."

"That is not a monster. I saw your mother when I found you. Remember? She's an old brown dog with white spots."

"Correction, she is a brown dog. And that is such a terrible shame that she's a brown dog while I'm something much more rarified."

"What are you, then?"

"A puppy. A singular puppy with a boon favor to ask."

"What?"

"If you kill my mother you can keep me forever."

"Forever and ever?"

"That is the deal."

"But dogs don't live forever, do they?"

"I'm not a dog, I'm a puppy. They're very different things. But I should make this much clear to you up front."

"Yes?"

"You won't live forever, just me. You'll just live a normal life and get to keep me forever."

"That's still a very long time. Almost forever."

"Yes it is." Panting cold emerged from Fredrick's pink tongue.

"Why can't you kill her?"

"Well, that's a very good question and I'm glad you're asking me hard questions. You see Joey, I'm just a puppy. You're a boy. Boys can kill so much more easily than puppies can."

"Easily?"

"So easily. And then I've barely had a month of breath and you've had eight summers of air inside your getting stronger by the by boy lungs."

Joey thought about this and it made sense. "We can't tell our parents."

"My parents are not your parents."

"Then how do I do it?"

"Let's shake on it like boon blood

28

brothers and then I'll fill you in."

Joey shook Fredrick's brown forepaw. Fredrick wagged his stubby tail. Fredrick's paw felt broken to Joey, and he doubted the puppy had bones.

"A promise is a promise," said Fredrick the white and brown puppy.

"Where we going?"

The puppy trailed ahead of Joey, zig-zagging, eager to lead.

"We're going to the edge of the world, then back. We're going to step off a cliff and laugh at the sun."

J oey crawled through the torn back screen window of Mrs. Bass's ramshackle house. Her neglected backyard was full of fallen tangerines and oranges, rotten and ripe. The cracker house smelled of tanned leather and baby food.

"Fredrick?"

Joey opened the back door for Fredrick to amble inside. After the door swung in, the torn screen window flapped out and sat still.

Fredrick tipped over the garbage can underneath the kitchen sink after several tries and ate the rotten food.

What would happen if Mrs. Bass discovered the pair ransacking her kitchen? She would call the police and have her looters arrested. And Joey could be jailed. Joey had once stood in Mrs. Bass's front yard holding one of her kittens upside down by the tail until Mrs. Bass yelled "What are you doing? You!"

Mrs. Bass had given all the kittens away and eventually the mother cat had died. Then Mrs. Bass switched to dogs. She liked dogs better because they listened. Yet all of her puppies had been given away. Fredrick had been the last, the runt of the litter.

Joey felt his weight creaking over the floorboards. Mrs. Bass was old. Joey wondered if Mrs. Bass would even know how to turn on a TV set if she saw one.

"There's food in the kitchen," Fredrick said.

"I'm not so hungry."

"But you are. Killing's hungry work. You should eat a Mallow Bar."

"Shouldn't we be underneath the house hunting it?"

"We were sent to kill the monster."

"Where?"

"Sleeping in her bedroom, fat and hot."

Joey walked down the hallway, one red shoelace untied, socks mis-matched.

"Did you know what they would call you in Australia?" Fredrick asked.

"Why didn't you bite off Darth Vader's head?"
"He used the force on me," Fredrick confessed.

29

"What?"

"A baby kangaroo."

Joey walked to the hallway's end and noticed how the mustard-colored paint was peeling off in bunches.

Mrs. Bass's bedroom was dimly lit, and Joey spied her, covered with pink and blue sheets like a fat wrinkled baby. Her limbs clung to the bed as if gravity was conspiring to pull her into her mound of sweaty pillows and make her the stuffing in the bed. Her false teeth sat gap-toothed and smiling on the nightstand. Joey looked up at the ceiling and pictured Mrs. Bass being stuck to it like a soiled hot air balloon.

"I can't kill her. She's the old widow lady."

"At first you think you can't. Yes you can. You can. You shook on it like a boon brother. Just this morning you did."

"Will it hurt much?"

"Quite a bit I imagine and yet I've never been killed."

"How?"

"Go to the bed and I'll tell you. "

"But I'll get in trouble."

"I'll tell you what. I'll be the fall guy."

"You'll what?"

"I'll get in trouble for your criminal negligence. Lift me up on the bed and if anyone wonders about it, they'll know a puppy killed the old lady, by my paw prints."

"But that's crazy. Puppies don't kill people."

"I do." Fredrick looked at Joey very carefully, considering.

"But why?"

"Well, you know how I have two names?"

"You have one name."

"No. I'm Fred and Rick. That's like being two different puppies. Since I have two different names I can act two different ways."

"I don't have that advantage, do I?"

"No, you don't. And what if I told you it wasn't me that wanted to do bad things but another smaller pup that lived inside of me that wanted to do bad things? Who would you blame it on, me, or the smaller pup that lived inside of me?"

Joey thought. "I guess I'd blame it on the smaller pup that lived inside of you."

"And what if that smaller pup blamed it on another smaller pup inside of him?"

"Then I guess it wouldn't be his fault either."

"Well, now you understand perfectly my dilemma." And Fredrick smiled just wide enough to show his fangs.

"But it would still be wrong," Joey insisted.

Fredrick growled at Joey's logic and then caught himself, and perked up instantly. "But what if you weren't really killing an old woman? What if inside the woman lived a much smaller woman, say a little girl?"

"Well . . ."

"Or an old shriveled up hag?"

"Mrs. Bass is an old shriveled up hag."

"Well of course she is, but I just mean an older more shriveled up hag that you don't know and don't care about."

"Oh."

Joey deposited Fredrick at the left edge of Mrs. Bass's bed. In many ways, Joey thought Fredrick was like any other puppy. And this was his first puppy; so maybe puppies ran the gamut in terms of activities they preferred. Maybe some puppies were just partial to killing old ladies in bed while they slept. That would explain a lot. Fredrick liked to smell and lick things. He plodded along the wrinkled flannel sheets and went to the old woman's bosom. He cocked his head to the side until his brown floppy ear turned over on itself like an elephant's. He kept his head turned to the side for several seconds as he listened to her heart pumping blood.

Satisfied, he dashed to the edge of the bed and Joey sat him back on the ground.

"Move to her bedside."

"Will I get in trouble?"

"Not from me."

"You can't get me in any trouble."

"That's a matter of opinion."

Joey walked to the side of Mrs. Bass's bed and looked down at her doubtfully.

"What now?"

"Kiss her."

"What?"

"Kiss her, full on the mouth."

But Mrs. Bass rolled away from Joey, onto her left side and snored.

It was willful disobedience.

Joey walked around to the other side of the bed, watching the dirty linen.

Joey's eyes met her starched and bloated face.

It occurred to Joey that this was a dubious first post-Mother kiss. His first post-Mom kiss would have to be revisited.

Joey's lips moved to Mrs. Bass's mouth. He closed his eyes and hoped for the best.

"Wait!" Fredrick snapped.

Joey shot his head back up.

"You have to kiss her until you feel her breath strangling you."

"Yes."

"Her breath is essence. Essence is life."

Joey pursed his lips together and moved his mouth down until his lips met Mrs. Bass's. Her lips felt awkward and wet like careless smiles in the dark. Her bedclothes smelled of gym class shoelaces dripping with honeyed molasses.

Joey was not practiced in the art. And as he moved his lips to her mouth he felt dog slobber dribbling down his mouth. He instinctively pulled away before catching himself.

Joey could feel hot breath moving through her belly like a stone beneath the surface. It pulsed, moving along warm and savory beneath his skin.

When her breath hit him, he had expended his, waiting for the inevitable.

Her aroma came into him with a sudden ferocity and Joey choked, unable to keep his own breath in, his hips falling away, bracing himself.

The puppy moved away from the bedside and the old woman was still.

Joey sighed. "You lied."

"And yet in a sense my statement was correct. She mothered my mother and by default that makes her my mother, or at least my grandmother."

As they walked by the old woman's possessions, passing yarn, dog food and old newspapers, Joey knew it would be the last time he visited her home.

"This house is ripe for the pickings," Fredrick said, looking at the low-hanging fruit on the old woman's orange trees through her green-tinted windows.

Joey stuffed a Mallow Bar carelessly into his jacket pocket.

J oey and his father watched as the paramedics carried Mrs. Bass out.

"Mrs. Bass wasn't even that old," Sam said.

32

Joey looked at his fingers.

"Who's going to live next door now?" Joey asked.

"Hell, I don't know."

Joey watched one of the paramedics mishandle the stretcher for just a second but managed to correct it before Mrs. Bass fell off and onto the gravel path.

He was lucky, Joey thought. It was not good to drop dead people. You should not drop a person who had lived quietly by herself and fed small animals as her only worldly pleasure.

"Do they put puppies to sleep?"

"No, they only put dogs to sleep. Fredrick will have to get a lot older before they can put him to sleep."

"I don't know if he'll have to get that much older before they do."

" Do you know exactly how I killed her?" Joey asked.

"You have little boy germs all over you. It makes me want to go and have a bath just thinking about you and your little boy germs."

"Do you want a bath?"

"Of course not."

Joey stared at Fredrick's antic form.

"And in her weakened state, little boy germs were enough to kill the monster."

"But that doesn't make any sense, Fredrick Brown."

"Yes it does."

"And don't you have puppy germs?"

"No."

"Nothing you say makes sense."

Joey scrubbed his hands clean in the sink that evening. He tried to give Fredrick a bath but the puppy growled in protest, baring his fangs. Growling, his eyes, pits of coal, reminded Joey of hornets.

Joey's paternal grandmother Quilty was staying with the Browns on Friday evening.

Joey kept miniature Star Wars figures in his room along with an X-Wing Fighter and TIE Fighter toy replicas.

"Oh, Joey," Gramma Quilty sighed, "but you're too old to be playing with dolls."

Joey had gone to a great deal of trouble collecting his Star Wars action figures and had really hoped Quilty would play with his Star Wars collection.

He hated how Gramma Quilty called his action figures dolls. Everyone knew dolls were for girls. He owned action figures, not dolls, which just went to show Gramma Quilty's truly doltish nature. Joey had once tried to explain the difference between dolls and action figures, but she just smiled and said "dear."

Joey had once saved up $2.73 in loose change to buy the Hasbro Han Solo action figure, but when he explained to his maternal grandparents about his effort to save $3.99, and told them how close he was to buying the action figure and would they make up the $1.26 difference plus tax, they purchased Han Solo. They let him keep his $2.73 in loose change. This surprised Joey. He never dreamed his other grandparents would let him keep the $2.73 and buy the action figure, giving him $3.99 plus tax as a gift. Now he could start saving up for C3PO. After he had left Sears it occurred to him he should have asked for C3PO as well.

"But I like Star Wars."

"But you're too old for dolls, dear. Too too old."

In the morning, Joey noticed the heads of all of his Star Wars figures had been bitten off except Darth Vader's helmet.

"You might be too old for them but I'm not," Fredrick said. He sat in a dark corner guarding his plastic Star Wars heads, growling at Joey's effort to reclaim them. "You're eight, that's an old man in dog years."

"But I have the bodies," protested Joey.

"But I have the heads."

"Why didn't you bite off Darth Vader's head?"

"He used the force on me," Fredrick confessed.

The Family Brown went on a bike ride the next day, absent Quilty away on a shopping trip. Buicks and Fords infrequently passed them by, cruising DeLand's 1978 suburbs.

Joey's mother Belinda cycled behind them, with Fredrick perched in the Schwinn carrier seat, happily panting.

Joey kept his legs raised up behind Sam and sat on the child's safety seat.

"Put your legs in the bike spokes," Fredrick said. "See what happens when your legs go broke inside the spokes!"

"That would hurt!"

"Broke inside the spokes! It certainly would. And more than just you. And that is why you should do it."

"I'll get in trouble again," Joey pleaded.

"You didn't bite the heads off your men."

"What?" Sam did not bother to turn around. Joey's father had difficulty hearing in his left ear since the Korean War. One of Sam's enlisted men had fired a service revolver too close to his head.

"See, he doesn't want you to know!" Fredrick barked.

"What else is he keeping from me?"

Screeching down the hill. Flying. Seeing the wheels whistle. Red Schwinn ten speed cruising down the hill.

34

Globbed onto the back of a bike seat eight years old like a fat beer nut. Wheels burning up the concrete. Paradise.

"Dad, what would happen if I stuck my foot in the bike spokes?"

"Just don't do it!" Sam's knuckles were painted white against the bike's red-rimmed handle bars.

Why withhold crucial information about biking etiquette? He lowered his foot into the circular abyss.

Blood. Curses. Long walk home and no wind blowing their hair. Mother was coasting along with one leg on the ground so they could keep up, looking back at them reluctantly like someone was following her home without her permission.

Joey had never seen his father bleed. Joey was crying but Sam was too mad to care. His mother looked at Joey like he was a dead boy. Fredrick was happy to scratch his butt.

"Why did you do that?" Sam asked him days later.

"You should have just told me," Joey wanted to say, but said nothing.

Fredrick was licking one of the many scratches on Sam's arm, teasing out the blood.

"Good boy," Sam said, as Fredrick licked his hand.

"Could a dog have a job?" Joey asked his mother.

"What a strange question. Do you know any dogs with jobs?" Belinda was washing lunch dishes.

"I think so."

"Which dog?"

"Fredrick."

"And what is Fredrick's job?"

Killing people, Joey started to say and then stopped. "I think being a vampire is Fredrick's job."

"And is being a vampire a job?"

"Well some people do it."

"For a living?"

"No-o. I guess not. As a hobby then?"

"No is right. I'm afraid Fredrick will always just be a dog."

Fredrick padded in, sniffing.

"And just look at him, Joey Brown. Wouldn't we know if Fredrick was a vampire? Really. He's just a cute little fur ball."

Fredrick begged with his forepaws and Belinda laughed at his antics.

"Am I crazy?" Joey asked Fredrick.

"Whenever you start to ask yourself that, turn it around and ask it about the other guy."

"Do lots of people's dogs talk to them?"

"I'm not a dog, I'm a puppy."

"I keep forgetting. You act so grown up."

"Also, if you were really crazy I'd be telling you to do really mean things. I always have you do nice things. Sane people don't hear nice voices. I want you to go donate some oranges to the homeless shelter."

"I suppose you have a point. That is a nice thing." Joey took a bag to gather up the rotten oranges from his back yard. It had been a hard freeze. The homeless would enjoy a nice bag full of oranges.

"Let's go tramping," Fredrick announced. They were in Joey's bedroom, playing with the headless Star Wars action figures on an imaginary Death Star. Joey had tried gluing the heads back on with Elmer's Glue but the heads kept falling off. He had better luck gluing the heads back to their chests and groins.

Fredrick was Darth Vader, the lone action figure with the head intact. Joey played headless C3PO. This indeed made sense, since C3PO was a robot and could lose his head and still function. He wasn't sure if he liked being C3PO, though. Sure, C3PO knew everything, but he could do nothing.

"Where?"

"Oh, just skylarking. Where we end up you'll never know. You should bring provisions for me. I mean, for us to eat."

Joey pillaged his parents' kitchen and

put a box of Chex cereal, Purina dry puppy chow and three warm cans of Coke into a brown Publix shopping bag.

Train tracks ran behind Joey's one-acre yard, past the orange trees, and nightly freight trains traversed the Brown's back yard between the rear of their orange grove and the packing warehouse.

Fredrick barked and Joey sat him down on the train tracks.

Fredrick crossed over the tracks, stumbling, happy outside. He shook his brown fur and trudged along as if pleasantly drunk.

"Do you ever play?" Joey asked.

"Why, that's what I'm doing right now. I'm playing. Can I tell you a secret?"

"Sure."

"I don't think I'm going to live for ever after all."

"No?"

"No."

"I have a feeling I won't live for ever either. And I wouldn't want to anyways."

"That's good. Nothing's better than two friends with a finite amount of time on their hands, spending it together."

"Yes," Joey agreed.

"Let's go for a ride."

"On the train?"

"Yes, tramping. Have you never tramped about?"

"No."

36

"No? What have you done with the eight years you've been given?"

"Things."

"Things, well."

"Won't they ask for train tickets?"

"Who needs tickets? Passengers don't ride the train. So since we're not allowed to ride the train we shouldn't need tickets."

"But that doesn't make any sense."

"Yes it does."

"Nothing you say ever makes sense."

"Then I hire you as a Red Line train employee."

"Can you just do that?"

"I just did."

Joey picked Fredrick up and deposited him inside the bed of the Red Line train. He sat the Publix bag next to Fredrick as the train started up. The Coke cans collided. Fredrick's fur was sticking up. The wheels picked up speed and grinded quickly against the tracks, building momentum.

"You have to hurry," Fredrick said. "You have to get on my train."

Joey was running then, shrieking, and trying to get his hands up high enough to climb aboard. He was running as fast as he could, Fredrick was eying him sympathetically, and yet Joey could not catch up.

"You have to help me," Joey shrieked. "You have to help me on the train!"

Fredrick cast his eyes down at the

fast-moving ground.

"Jump down!" Joey pleaded, crying. "You have to jump down or I'll lose you." He was shouting at the world, and Fredrick seemed to want to jump down and yet he sat patiently, eyeballs puddles of mud.

"I can't," Fredrick said. "I'll hurt myself. Terribly."

Fredrick barked for Joey to hurry his little boy legs, but Joey was slow. Joey had always been a slow boy. He could see Fredrick riding away in the train, looking smaller as the locomotive picked up steam.

Disappearing, Fredrick squeaked: "It wasn't really the little dog inside me." And then he became a small black dot squared into negative infinity backwards.

Joey could feel Fredrick slipping away from him but it did not quite feel real. It felt as if all the fairness and beauty had been banished as the Red Line train flew away. The locomotive disappeared, blowing steam. It was as if he had never found Fredrick in the house next door.

Joey walked home, wondering how he would explain Fredrick's absence. It occurred to him his parents would not bother to ask what happened to the puppy. It was not that they were careless; it was just one less mouth to feed.

Joey and his parents ate spaghetti drenched in Ragu meat sauce held together with shaken Parmesan cheese.

"Mr. Watson called today from your school. He wanted to talk about something you've been bringing to school with you," Sam said.

"I don't want to talk about that now."

"You should have some friends over sometime, Honey," Belinda said.

"Yeah, maybe." Joey imagined this would be an easier prospect if he had friends. Fredrick was his only friend. Thinking about Fredrick's absence, he felt like sticking the table fork's points into his open palm to allow the blood to drain out of his hand. He would wordlessly leave the table and in his room pull apart the limbs from his Star Wars action figures one joint at a time. And he would scream "Fredrick!" after every limb he pulled off.

And he would defy Gramma Quilty to tell him that he was too old for Star Wars action figures. And if she dared to say "dolls" he would take limbless C3PO and hold it up in her face screaming, "Does this look like a doll to you, Gramma?"

Joey was woken up that night by a peculiar scratching on his bedroom floor.

It was the soft scuffling noise scurrying rats make.

He could faintly hear something being pushed along the surface of his wooden floor.

Scratching slowly against the wood, being bumped along.

Joey climbed out of bed, barely awake. Something nipped at his heel. He screamed.

He flicked on the light.

"Fredrick!" he screamed joyfully.

Fredrick was pushing a train conductor's cap along the floor with some difficulty.

"How did you get back?"

"Oh, I stopped the train."

"You didn't hurt anyone, did you?"

"Well, not on purpose, but I did what I needed to do to come back."

"For me?"

"All for you, Joey. Everything's always been for you."

"But how did you get the conductor's hat?"

"Oh, the Red Line conductor won't need it anymore."

"Fredrick, what did you do?" Joey noticed a dried brown splotch on the blue and white conductor's hat.

"I did what I needed to get back to you."

"But . . ."

"You didn't want me to stay on the train, did you?"

"But . . ."

38

"Now, did you?"

"Here, you can sleep with me."

In the morning, Sam read the DeLand Sun News at the breakfast table, hanging over his toast and eggs like an oversized menu.

"Morning."

"Morning."

Joey poured himself milk and juice and fixed a piece of buttered toast.

"Anything happen?"

"A freight train wrecked." The wreck had made the paper's cover.

"Was anyone hurt?"

"Just everyone on the train. Cereal?"

"Yeah, Cocoa Puffs with lots of milk."

After breakfast, Joey and Fredrick went walking in the orange grove.

"Fredrick, this has to stop."

"The train did stop." Joey caught Fredrick smiling. Sometimes he could catch the puppy smiling a wicked grin if he was just quick enough. It wasn't very often. "It isn't the end of trains." They walked through the orange grove and onto the train tracks.

"You have to stop hurting people."

"Oh, you mean that. You just mean the people."

"Yes of course I mean the people."

"People are always getting hurt. You can just pick up a paper and read about it every day. It's boring, really."

"Fredrick, stop it!"

"Well, I did have an idea."

"What?"

"That we could stop, I could stop committing crimes and start solving them."

"You mean, be the good guys?"

"Precisely."

"Like on the cartoons? Like the Justice League?"

"Just like them. Spy secrets and stuff. It would be a lark preventing nuclear wars."

"What's a lark?"

"You needn't concern yourself with that, Master Brown. You would be my boon companion that gets rescued in every single episode. Or killed at the end. My choice."

Joey saw a girl his age walking west towards them on the tracks. She wore a pink gingham dress. The girl was in Joey's third grade class and blinked often. She looked like she wanted to close her eyes but they kept blinking.

"Looks like we're on a collision course," Jenny Kurtz said.

"Hey."

"You're in my class, aren't you?"

"Yeah."

"You're the boy who doesn't talk."

"Yeah."

"You seem to talk OK now."

"Yeah."

"What's that?"

She pointed at Fredrick.

"That's just my dog."

"What's a matter with him?"

"Nothing's wrong with him."

"Then why's he not moving?"

"He is."

"No he's not, silly."

Joey looked down and saw Fredrick was lying on his back with four paws up in the air.

"I think he's dead." Jenny Kurtz tapped Fredrick with the toe of her patent leather saddle shoe. "You should know better than to play with a dead dog."

"Fredrick!" Joey snapped. "Get up!" Nothing. "Fredrick I mean it!"

"I'm gonna get help."

"Why?" He thought he caught Fredrick winking at him when Jenny turned her head back in the direction of her house.

"Listen: your dog is dead."

"He's not dead."

The Kurtz girl kicked Fredrick again, this time harder. "Yeah, he's really dead."

"He does that sometimes. Playing for my attention."

"Sure."

Joey followed the Kurtz girl home. "He's been playing with a dead dog, Mom."

"He's a puppy."

Mrs. Kurtz told Jenny's older sister Marlys to take a look at Joey's dog. "But be careful of rabies."

"What's rabies?" Joey asked.

"It's when a dog bites people and stays cross all the time," Marlys said. "Don't you know anything?"

Marlys had been talking on the phone to her girlfriend Joanie and eating Doritos before her kid sister came home. She was not very happy to end her conversation with Joanie and quit eating Doritos. She did not want to look at a boy's dead dog on the railroad tracks. She wore pink flip-flops, Lee Blue Jeans and a tank top. She was almost six feet tall and big boned.

"So how did your dog get it?" Marlys asked. She was chewing a mouthful of Doritos and Joey had difficulty understanding her.

"Get what?" They went back outside.

"Are you deaf? Where's your dead dog, kid?"

"He's not dead. We're going to solve crimes together and stuff."

"Is this kid stupid or something?" Marlys pointed to her left ear and made a circular motion with her right index finger.

"He doesn't talk in school."

"Doesn't talk? What's wrong with you, kid?"

Joey frowned. They were almost at the tracks. He thought Marlys's buttocks were enormous and he wanted to stop looking at her rear because her pink thong underwear kept poking out from inside her Lee Blue Jeans.

"See, I told you. He just frowns and

40

makes that face."

"Well, listen kid. When we find your dog you can't touch it. Even if it's dead it might have heartworms, and believe me you don't want to get heartworms."

"Heartworms?" Joey's nose crinkled.

"It's a bug that crawls inside your heart and gives you a heart attack. And if you ever get one, you should call 911. Heartworm's more dangerous than a nuke."

"What's a nuke?" Joey whispered.

"Do you even know what the Cuban Missile Crisis is?" Marlys laughed. "God, you're fun!"

"No, I don't smoke." He had once heard his father mention good Cuban cigars.

"No, I don't smoke! You crack me up!" Marlys howled. "Don't you know that the Ruskies want to nuke us? Our dad works for the state department, and they tell him secrets. They transmit codes to him on a portable radio."

"Could a dog hear them?" Joey asked.

"Sure, but not a dead dog. Sorry, kid."

"She takes the bus to high school," Jenny Kurtz explained.

They arrived at the spot where they had been, but Fredrick was missing.

"Somebody threw your dead dog away, kid. Get used to people throwing your stuff away."

Joey looked around with a vacant expression.

"I think he's in shock," Marlys said. "How old was your dog, kid?"

"Two."

"Two years old! That's too young for heartworms."

"Two months old."

"Is this kid special ed?"

"He's in the same class I am. I think he's gifted."

"That would explain a lot. Gifted kids are more screwed up than the retards. What happened to your arms kid?"

"I fell off my bike."

"Do your parents beat you, kid?"

"No."

"God. If I had a gifted kid like you I'd beat you with a two by four."

"OK."

"God, is that all you say is OK?"

"No."

"God, what a kid. Gifted! Jenny, be home for dinner."

"Sure."

Marlys stalked off, looking back at Joey twice in exasperation, moving her arms a lot as she walked.

"What do you want to do?" Jenny said.

"Look for Fredrick."

"But he's dead."

"He was only playing."

"I read about how animals, when they're hurt and ready to die, they'll go off to be by themselves."

Joey thought this meant they were smarter than people.

"Jenny, if you knew someone was doing something bad, would you tell on him?"

"It would depend."

"I mean bad things. Really bad things."

"I suppose."

"But what if you thought no one would believe you?"

"At least you would have tried."

"Yeah, well."

"Who are you talking about, that kid who smacks you in the head every day?"

"No, not Franklin."

"Oh."

"Jenny?"

"Yeah?"

"You're talking to me now, but will you still talk to me when we're back in Mrs. Pemberton's class?"

"Yeah, I guess. If you talk to me."

"Yeah, I will."

"Have you ever gone tramping before, Jenny?"

"No, not here."

"Skylarking?"

"I don't even know what that is."

"Then what?"

"I thought it would be fun to sit here and talk."

"Yeah."

"Do you know what some of the other girls said about you?"

"What's that?"

"They said you must be a foreign

41

exchange student."

"They did?" Joey scratched his head and blinked several times.

"Oh yes. Some of them said you were from Albania. Were you held back?"

"Held back from what?"

"In school. Held back in school."

"Not that I know of. Probably not."

"You'd know if you were held back. Marlys was held back and that's why she's mad at everyone."

"It must be bad to be held back."

"It sucks monkey grapes. That's what Marlys said. This sucks monkey grapes."

"Does she ever beat you up?"

"No, she only likes to beat up boys. And she's bigger because she was held back. So she can. I'm surprised she didn't beat you up."

"Maybe she liked me."

"No."

"Do you have any animals?"

"I have a sad cat."

"Why's she sad?"

"Because she's a cat. Aren't you sad that you're a boy?"

"Maybe now that you've said it."

"I mean because that's all you'll ever be is a boy who doesn't say very much."

"Well, has your cat ever killed anyone?"

"That would really be something, Joey Brown."

"Yeah."

"I never saw Jasmine kill anything, but my mom says she brings dead birds

42

to our door, and it reminded her of this Alfred Hitchcock movie she once saw."

"What Alfred Hitchcock movie?"

"I don't remember. I've only seen two movies, and I don't think it was either of them."

"Did you see Star Wars?"

"Yes."

"Who's your favorite character?"

"The old man with the sword."

"That's Obi Wan, and it's a light saber."

"Yes."

"Animals are bad sometimes, aren't they? I mean, sometimes if they get angry, they just can't help but kill, can they?"

"That sounds like you're making up excuses for animals."

"Yeah."

Joey could see Jasmine slinking along the tracks towards them, rubbing her sides along the rusted bars, a sad chestnut cat.

Joey and Jenny Kurtz sat off to the side of the tracks on the concrete embankment, listening to a train approach.

Jasmine jumped up on Jenny's lap and meowed.

"Oh, quiet Jasmine."

"I would never tell Fredrick to be quiet."

"She's telling stories again. She says there's an insane puppy loose on this block, and he's plotting to start a world war. He's a master of disguise. He's going to work as a KGB double agent and sell them all our dad's defense codes for a dollar."

"That's a good joke. Can't Jimmy Carter catch the puppy?"

Jasmine meowed.

"He's trying his best, but the puppy knows more about nukes and espionage than even Jimmy Carter does," Jenny translated.

"Is she joking?"

"No, never. That's why she's so sad. Right now this puppy's selling codes to the Russians for a dollar. He thinks a dollar is a lot of money."

"Isn't it a lot?"

"I guess. When he sells all our codes, they'll nuke us cold."

"Does she know a way out?"

Jasmine meowed.

"The puppy has brothers and sisters. Some of them were good. But then again, some of them were also bad. They're making their own plans and they don't concern our world." Jenny stood looking at Joey as if she wanted him to speak.

"Fredrick was the runt of the litter." Joey closed his eyes. He kissed Jenny on the cheek, and then the lips. "That was better alright."

Jenny's mouth held the perfect O shape of a tart navel orange.

"Better than what?" Jenny Kurtz said, suddenly jealous.

"A whole lot better than kissing the dead lady!" Joey's lips moved to Jenny's mouth as the last Blue Line Train coasted down the rusted tracks.

————————————————

43

Alexa Chats... with Mike Allen
by Alexandra Seidel

AS: Mike, now is the time to brag a little; please introduce yourself to our readers.

MA: It's hard to explain the full scope of what I do, but I'll give it a shot. In my day job, I'm the arts columnist for *The Roanoke Times*, the daily newspaper where I've worked for 13 years. Outside that, I write fiction. I've had more than 30 stories appear in mostly well-out-of-the-way places over the past 20 years, though one of them, a horror tale called "The Button Bin," was a Nebula Award finalist in 2009. And I write poetry. I've had more than 200 poems see print; three of them have won the Rhysling Award for speculative poetry. Also, one of my poetry collections, *Strange Wisdoms of the Dead*, was picked as an Editor's Choice selection by *The Philadelphia Inquirer*. I also edit poetry and fiction. I make selections for both the anthology series *Clockwork Phoenix*, which is at the moment between publishers, and my little poetry journal, *Mythic Delirium*, for which I'm also publisher. I'm a volunteer for the Interstitial Arts Foundation. There's other things, but those are the major

threads.

AS: You said in an interview that you "began *Mythic Delirium* back in 1998 as sort of a self-dare"*. What did you want to prove?

MA: I'd attempted a couple editing/publishing ventures in partnership with others, and wound up unhappy, for different reasons each time. So the dare was to show I could attempt a publishing venture completely on my own and make it work. Curiously, that's not how it panned out. *Mythic Delirium* went nowhere fast until DNA Publications picked it up. I think I remain the only speculative poetry editor lucky enough to have had my zine produced and paid for under the umbrella of a major house. Yet when DNA collapsed in the mid-90s, I wound up going it alone after all. And it's worked, but I still have to doff my hat to DNA for elevating *Mythic Delirium* to a position where it could hold its own.

AS: You have been doing the 'poetry thing' for quite some time, both as an editor and as a poet. What changes have you seen in subject matter and

in how poets work with it over the years?

MA: For the sake of space I'll oversimplify. I've seen more poems and more poets interested in exploring folkloric and mythological themes, both inside and outside Western culture. Woman writers are at the core of this, and I've seen their ranks noticeably increasing. I've seen more writers of color interested in creating speculative poems that speak to their experience. I've seen people tackling speculative poetry, and letting their work appear in spec poetry venues, whose interest stems primarily from the literary/poetry tradition rather than the sf/fantasy tradition, and who have ambitions of crafting work that holds up to the best in both realms. I don't recall much discussion of any of these issues in the late 1990s, which was when I first found solid footing on the poetry slope.

AS: **When you say there are more women writers and writers of color in the spec poetry field (the lack of which has been criticized elsewhere in the genre) you are certainly right. What makes the sf/f poetry field so much more open to minorities?**

MA: I'm not sure I'm comfortable framing this in terms of sf/f poetry being innately more open. There's a perception that the sf poetry field, or at least a portion of it, has not been interested in encouraging viewpoints that don't mesh with what's culturally dominant. Rose Lemberg's excellent new online venue *Stone Telling* was at least in part a response to this.

What I think might be true is that the field as a whole is more inclined to self-examination, more aware of its deficiencies, less inclined to be insular, than it used to be, and that has to do with more people finding out speculative poetry exists and trying their hand at it.

AS: **You told us about the changes you saw in the spec poetry field so far, where do you think those poets are going?**

MA: I think all these trends I mentioned will continue to expand. But there are many spec poets who just do their own thing, unaffected by any trend, and will keep doing it till they drop. So nothing you might like or dislike about how speculative poetry is presented today is going to disappear.

I would love to see speculative poetry produce a giant, someone whose effect on pop culture cannot be denied. Can that ever happen? We shall see.

AS: Poetry is not something readers are generally after (or so it seems), but especially in the speculative field, writers of prose often try their hand at poetry as well, J.R.R. Tolkien to name just one popular example, and there are distinct lyrical tendencies in speculative prose these days. Do you see a change in the perception of spec poetry, a change in readership?

MA: I think your typical reader has no idea speculative poetry exists (or if they do, they have wild misconceptions about what it is) and that the biggest audience for it remains the community of speculative poets. That, however, is larger, more interesting, and overall more inclusive than it was ten years ago. I think young writers like Catherynne Valente who crack the *New York Times* bestseller list and yet remain passionately vocal about writing, publishing and promoting poetry have given the scene a vital dose of new gravitas.

AS: What made you run for the Science Fiction Poetry Association Presidency back in '04?**

MA: To be blunt, I started volunteering for the organization in 2003, got an inside look at how poorly it was being run and realized that with even a minimal effort I could do much better. SFPA was failing at even the most basic things, like maintaining a website, putting out its newsletter, presenting itself as an organization worth being part of. My declaration for office resulted in the only contested election in SFPA's history to date -- which I won in a landslide.

AS: Looking back at your achievements as SFPA's President, which of them is the most important one to you?

MA: First, let me make clear: none of those achievements were mine alone. A lot of good people helped. A number of dedicated volunteers put in just as many crazy hours as I did. A lot of cool things happened when I was Prez. I think if I have an achievement to be proud of, it's that I helmed the turnaround; encouraged the association to take pride in and even flaunt its three decades of history, and also to be as welcoming to newcomers as possible. I did have setbacks. Debbie Kolodji, who took over after me, carried those efforts even further. And she also had setbacks. I hope her successors keep steering things in the best direction, despite whatever setbacks arise.

AS: Not only are you the editor of *Mythic Delirium*, your *Clockwork Phoenix* series is also quite a success. How is editing poetry different from editing short stories?

MA: The selection processes aren't really much different in either case. Anita, my wife, gives me feedback and arranges sequences the stories or poems could go in. I try to pick pieces that will compliment each other. And so on. Many more people submit to the fiction market than to the poetry market, but the poets submit multiple items, so it kind of balances out. I suppose, if there's a difference, it's that it's often easier for me to get my mind around what's not working for me in a story than it is for a poem, though with both forms it all comes down to gut instinct.

AS: In your experience, do poets and writers of fiction deal with different topics even inside the sf/f genre or are the same issues important but in a different way?

MA: Same topics and issues, different (yet overlapping) medium. I will say I think speculative poetry is often the follower rather than the leader in tackling difficult subjects. I'd love to be convinced otherwise.

AS: Tell us what interstitial arts

means for you, please.

MA: I define it in the broadest possible terms because being more specific defeats the purpose. It's any artistic expression that can't be easily squeezed into a familiar category. Interestingly, I think that's the way fine art is trending --- here in Roanoke it seems that every time I turn around one of the museums is installing a new exhibition that mixes video with painting with rock music with fashion with sculpture with ... Right now, I see the Interstitial Arts Foundation as having the task of pointing folks at a phenomenon which has already arrived but which few have a word for yet. It's

47

best though if you look for yourself and form your own ideas. The IAF can be found at interstitialarts.org.

AS: **You are known to perform your poetry on stage. Describe your ideal performance and the sort of poem you would perform?**

MA: I don't know what my "ideal" would be. I can give examples of how I've done it --- my Rhysling Award winner "The Strip Search" was written for stage, and that involves me pantomiming the step through Hell's gate and what happens afterward while I recite the poem. Another poem, "The Dream Eaters," which has only appeared in print in *Strange Wisdoms of the Dead*, involved me reading the piece as the lights gradually dimmed, which the help of two actresses dressed as demons, who ripped the verses from my hand and ate them (they were printed on rice paper.) With other poems, such as "Requited," I've used a pre-recorded track, which frees me and another actor (in this instance, my wife) to "illustrate" the piece. Often times I experiment with staging and lighting that hopefully amps up whatever's there. But then again, sometimes I just pace back and forth, reading from a sheet of paper. I think a lot of my poems work naturally as monologues.

AS: **Writing poetry to be performed on stage suggests that you write with an audience in mind. What can you tell us about your ideal reader?**

MA: You know, I don't think that way. I might, at most, aim a piece at a particular editor I know. And of course I love it when a piece of mine connects with an audience. But as for picturing some ideal reader? I dunno. I don't know if such a person even exists for what I write.

AS: **Victor Hugo said: "The guilty one is not he who commits the sin, but the one who causes the darkness." Would you agree that Hugo's idea can sometimes be found in your own writing? If so, where does that come from?**

MA: I think that phrase can certainly be applied to my writing, especially the fiction. There's a pervasive theme in at least some of my stories about the lengths a person will go to protect themselves from the knowledge of having committed a horrible act. "The Button Bin" perhaps codified it most clearly. There are two monsters in the story. The first is frightening from the outset. The revelation of the identity of the second is what provides the story's knife twist.

Some of this comes from having been a crime reporter, seeing the extremes of compartmentalization and rationalization that people engage in when they've done something that's unconscionable. Some of this comes from the darkest times of my childhood and adolescence, when I faced both violent abuse at home and violent bullying in school, and the terrible emotional monster that birthed, that sense that something must be wrong with me, even if it's something I don't understand, to bring these things down on myself.

AS: You said: "...and the terrible emotional monster that birthed, that sense that something must be wrong with me, even if it's something I don't understand, to bring these things down on myself." If you're comfortable sharing this, what helped you realize that these things were not internal, nothing you brought down on yourself? Where did that realization take you?

MA: Frankly, that sort of thing, you never get over. You just deal with it. I will say, I didn't start becoming comfortable (to the degree I ever will be) with myself until college. My then-girlfriend, now-wife had/has a lot to do with that.

AS: Looking at what you said before, I'm wondering about your choice to become a crime reporter. Was it

choice? How much of it was conscious, again, if you are comfortable answering?

MA: The jobs opened up -- I've held three different positions that involved crime coverage -- they were steps up the ladder, I took them. I can't really say if there was anything deeper involved.

AS: What goals are you pursuing in your writing career at the moment? Is there anything you want to achieve, you know, someday?

MA: As of this writing, I've more than halfway through the second draft of my first novel, a dark Appalachian Gothic full of talking animals, neurotic (or psychopathic) people and explosive violence. I'm also pushing myself to do less volunteering and produce more fiction overall. I've written a sequel to "The Button Bin" called "The Quiltmaker," and I can promise that the people who reviled the first story will really hate the second one. Mind you, I say that with pride.

Honestly, there's nothing I want to achieve "someday." I want it all now. But when you do it all, that's not so easy to pull off, hee.

AS: I'm sure that there is at least one more question I should have asked you, for example...?

MA: How about, where to find my work, especially as it's not always easy to find? The best starting point is my recently upgraded homepage, www.descentintolight.com. There's a poem I'm really proud of, "The King of Cats, the Queen of Wolves," co-written with Sonya Taaffe and Nicole Kornher-Stace, that appeared not long ago in *Apex Magazine*--where "The Button Bin" also has been reprinted. So far this year I've been in two anthologies: my novelette "Sleepless, Burning Life" can be found in JoSelle Vanderhooft's *Steam Powered: Lesbian Steampunk Stories*, and my short story "The Music of Bremen Farm" was reprinted in T.J. McIntyre's *Southern Fried Weirdness: Reconstruction*, a charity anthology to benefit the Red Cross. Other new poems are out or upcoming in *Apex, Ideomancer, Illumen, Inkscrawl, Bull Spec, Not One of Us, Strange Horizons* and ... *Fantastique Unfettered****.

AS: Thank you, Mike, for talking with me!

MA: Thank you, Alexa!

*The Mumpsimus, A Conversation With Mike Allen,
31 October 2005,
http://www.mumpsimus.blogspot.com/2005/10/conversation-with-mike-allen.html
** http://www.sfpoetry.com/
***Keep your eyes peeled for FU #4!

The Cartographer's Ache
by
Robert E. Stutts
For JQA

"Cartography gave Cook the long view, that we are shaped more by absence than by presence." ~Pamela Ball

Cities rise up between us,
then countries, continents, oceans:
I cannot get back to you now,
even if you weren't moving
away

My sense of direction has fragmented;
now only overlays of you
remain within me --
how I could never explore enough
your body's topography,
the contour of your curving
peninsula, the latitude
of salt on your nape,
the archipelago of your kisses
-- all conspire to keep me
lost

I too am my own map,
my edges worn:
my cartography used to unfold
readily at your touch,
like a shipwrecked sailor
whom luck or fate returns
to his home shore

At the edge of this world
on the palimpsest of my skin
reads the warning
here be dragons
(though they sleep)

Two Steps Forward

by

Sandra Odell

Herein, The Way.

Kinsey slit the throat of the last manaque as he spied the wanderer coming down the Way. The man was big, oak tree big, with thick limbs that ate up the distance sprouting from a heavy trunk of a body.

He kept a suspicious eye out while stripping the bodies of anything useful with the efficiency of need. The scrawny man-apes had the funk of wet burlap and rotting grass, but stench or no he was alive and they weren't. Kinsey pulled the three dead manaques off to the side and palmed a knife in case the big man insisted he share the wealth.

The man continued to close the distance with sure, even steps beneath the carnation pink sky. His clothes looked to be in good condition under the dust and miles, so did the sawed-off shotgun riding low on his right hip and the machete on his left peeking from under the duster with every step. A rucksack hitched over his left shoulder and Way-worn boots finished out the

gear, nice and all Kinsey decided but not worth a scrap after the tussle with the manaques.

Twenty-seven.

Twenty-eight.

Twenty-nine.

The stranger passed by at thirty steps. He didn't slow, paying Kinsey's treasures half a breath without breaking stride. No reason to give him a second thought, yet as the man passed by Kinsey noticed a distance in his expression and it set him to thinking thoughts like *did years or miles set the lines around his mouth?*, and *how'd he come to miss an earlobe?* The common sense of survival told Kinsey to keep to himself, but loneliness had a voice of its own and to his surprise he heard himself say, "Hey, you want some?"

The wanderer stopped and turned on his heel. "Pardon?"

Straight on, the first thing Kinsey noticed was the guy's nose; it squatted in the middle of his face like a warty toad, a mangled tribute to one too many fights. As Kinsey's mother would have said, there wasn't anything else to the man's face to ease the eyes. His dark curls had only passing knowledge of clippers and his chin too wide for appeal, but his eyes were the color of old ash and sharp in their attention.

Kinsey rose slowly as he held out a leathery strip of meat. "Jerky. Want some? It should be good, um, so long as there ain't any teeth or stuff."

The wanderer kept still. "Sure." Something like amusement lurked behind the word.

Kinsey waited and when the stranger still didn't move he dared a step forward. "Um, here. They didn't have much, the manaques I mean."

The man cut a look at the three ravaged corpses as he accepted the offering. "I bet." The jerky disappeared beneath the coat.

"Hey, what can I say? They thought I was an easy mark when I was dozin'. So, um, good to meet you. I'm Kinsey Morris." He almost offered his right hand before realizing it was the one with the knife, and kept it at his side.

The wanderer looked Kinsey up and down in the way of strangers in strange places. "Brahn," he said eventually.

"Brahn. That's it, huh? Just Brahn?"

"Yeah." The man showed Kinsey his back and continued down the Way.

Kinsey hadn't realized how much he missed the sound of someone else's voice until it left him behind. He could spare another piece or three of jerky for a chance to talk to someone other than himself. He hurried to catch up. "Not that I care. I mean, it's your name, right?" He stuffed his hands in the pockets of his threadbare camouflage jacket, slipping the knife back into its sheath through the hole in the lining. "Where ya from?"

"Around."

The wind picked up as they walked, breathing life into streamers of pale purple and mustard clouds. Kinsey

Something tight twisted in Kinsey's gut as he caught sight of the townsfolk's milky white eyes, but he figured his red hair and thick splash of hometown freckles might look as strange to them. Kinsey kept a smile on his face and his hands in plain sight, relieved Brahn did the same.

found he had to skip step to keep up with the wanderer. "Yeah, I guess it don't matter much any more, huh? I mean, we ain't in Kansas any more, are we, huh? I'm from, um, St. Paul; it's the one in Minnesota."

"I've heard of it."

"St. Paul's a great place," Kinsey said, "or was a great place, I haven't been there in a while, y'know? There was this burger shop called Humphrey's that had the best – hey, can we slow down a bit?"

The even steps stuttered, allowing Kinsey to catch up. "Anyway, they had the best bacon cheeseburgers; they used pepper bacon and some kinda tartar sauce instead of ketchup."

"Mm-hmmm."

"Want some more jerky?"

"No," Brahn said.

"It should be okay."

"That's what you said."

The Way went on, and so did they.

They made camp as the suns stole towards the mountains in the direction Kinsey had come to think of as West.

Brahn angled off the road to the left at a fairly flat stretch. Deciding the place looked as good as any, Kinsey followed, and together they gigged the ground until they were certain nothing lurked expectantly beneath the surface. By the time Kinsey shed his gear and checked his blades, Brahn had sparked a cook fire to life. The flames whispered teal blue in the coming rose dark and cast no shadows.

Dinner was the revenant jerky steeped in two tin cups of water off the boil and a handful of dark gold nuts Brahn dropped into the cups shell and all. A chunk of sharp yellow cheese from Brahn's pack completed the hobo's feast. They ate without speaking. Kinsey decided the big man wasn't much for dinner talk.

In time, Kinsey did the courteous turn of scrubbing out the cups with sand and a few more drops of water before setting them to dry by the fire. "So, where d'ya think we are?" he said as he dropped a spiny twig on the fire.

Brahn made an offering of his own. "Beats me, Roy."

"Huh?"

"Never mind."

"If you say so. I mean, um, do you ever think about where we are?"

Brahn bundled up his duster and stuck it under his head as he stretched out, settling his knotty shoulders on the sandy ground. "Not really."

"I do. Sometimes. I mean, not as much as I used to, but, um, just sometimes." Kinsey searched for stars in the empty sky; on nights like this, he had to admit he wasn't sure he remembered what a star looked like. He forgot more often than he remembered, anymore. There was a time when such things bothered him, but he didn't care much unless thoughts of his grandfather and Alzheimer's made his thinking crowded. Times like that were made for talking, even to himself. "Like, the last thin' I remember was brushin' my teeth. I used to work graveyard at the paper mill, so I'd come home an' get ready for bed because I never had any trouble sleepin' durin' the day, y'know? I brushed my teeth when it was a blue

58

sky outside, an' when I woke up, well, the sky wasn't blue an' I wasn't in my apartment. Freaked me out for a while there."

"Mmmm."

"What about you?"

Brahn held his peace for a time, eyes closed. "What about me?" The words were still, covered.

"Um, y'know, do you ever think about where we are now?"

Flames whispered, the wind called, and time snaked through the night. Brahn didn't answer. Kinsey fidgeted by the fire, wondering how to appease the terrible silence that had crystallized between them. "No hard feelin's; I was just askin'."

He barely heard Brahn's low sigh: "Yeah."

"So, um, where ya headin'?"

The big man shifted, and tucked the tips of his fingers under his belt. "I have no idea."

"But you'll know it when y'get there, huh? I heard about that place."

That brought something more like a smile to Brahn's lips, and Kinsey heard the crystal silence crack when the big man said, "Something like that, yeah."

"Even when you say somethin', you don't talk much, y'know that?"

Again there was that attempt at a smile. "I figured you talk enough for the both of us."

Kinsey plumped his knapsack for a pillow and turned to the fire though the night was warm enough without it. He tucked a knife into the sand as he watched Brahn through the flames, an uneven stretch of coming shadows on the far side of a fire with no shadows of its own.

People, human looking people, were few and far between on the Way. Brahn was the first he'd seen in. . .come to think of it, he couldn't recall ever having seen another human person on the Way. Kinsey's boyish humanity had cost him more than one night's stay in the rare settlements dotting the endless stretch of alien road. He often wondered if the mongrel residents saw in him the best of what they were before the change and could not bear to be reminded.

Kinsey liked people; loneliness wasn't much for conversation. "I've never been to I have no idea," he said as the flames settled to murmuring coals, "but I suppose I'd know it if I saw it."

Brahn shrugged into the sand. "The Way's big enough for both of us."

Kinsey nodded to himself and the night. "See you in the mornin'?"

"I suppose."

Kinsey dozed, waiting for a dream, and jerked awake at a word. He opened his eyes. Brahn lay on the other side of the fire, unmoving, eyes closed. "What?"

"I'm from Gatlinburg," Brahn said

59

quietly. "I lived there until I was ten, and then my parents pulled up stakes and moved the family to Chicago."

The unexpected comfort of an answer stayed with Kinsey until he fell asleep once more.

It was not so much a town as a clutch of low, desperate buildings huddled along the side of the Way in rationalized safety. Buckled rooftops glared morosely at the pink sky, and rough square garden patches drew the line in the sand against the orange bristle grass extending to the horizon. Better to eke out what meager existence could be had along the lunatic fringe than to brave the unknown, the place seemed to say.

Kinsey heard that, but he also heard the call to barter. "C'mon, what's to worry?"

"I don't like towns," Brahn said again from their perch on the far side of the hill overlooking the withered settlement.

Kinsey rolled up from his stomach to sit cross-legged on the side of the Way. "I mean, they look to be okay. They even got kids!"

"So do goats, that doesn't mean I want to talk to 'em."

"It'll be fine. We been watchin' them for three days now. They ain't done nothin' strange, um, nothin's come

down the Way. . ."

Brahn came up to a crouch, carefully positioning first his right foot then his left beneath him. "Towns get complicated."

Kinsey had no idea what the big man meant, but wasn't about to let that come between him and a chance at a for-real cooked meal, maybe even fresh water. "You an' me, we can manage it fine. Besides, we need some stuff. That last pack of manaques hit us real hard." Only five shells remained for the shotgun after the ambush seven days ago, a fact neither man could afford to ignore. "We don't gotta stay. We can be gone by nightfall if y'like."

Brahn moved like a mountain but eventually did move, coming to his feet and rolling his shoulders with slow deliberation as he considered the town. "Okay." The word rumbled like the birth of an avalanche. "Let's get it over with."

Kinsey was up in a flash, unzipping his camouflage jacket and checking the lay of his blades. "That's the spirit!" He started to jog down the hill, saying as he did, "Um, I got some of the jerky left. What about the screws from those four-armed things?"

He started out ahead of Brahn coming down the hill, yet Kinsey slowed and fell into step beside the larger man as they approached the mud and stripwood buildings. Dust and sweat

60

marked the boundaries of the town and with it a stench of abandoned hope that the wind of the grasslands could not dispel. Thready ferns stitched along the fronts of the houses served as the final resting place for discarded husks and neglected baubles: a wooden Popsicle stick with a faded riddle printed on one side; a dented kazoo; a pink plastic doll's body with no head; a strand of cracked blue beads. The residents jammed into doorways and watched their passing in silence. Skin and bone children crouched between the legs of adults, peeking from beneath the hems of their mother's dresses, studying the newcomers around the saggy legs of their fathers' pants.

Something tight twisted in Kinsey's gut as he caught sight of the townsfolk's milky white eyes, but he figured his red hair and thick splash of hometown freckles might look as strange to them. Kinsey kept a smile on his face and his hands in plain sight, relieved Brahn did the same. "Hey'all." He let his words carry in a smooth, easy tone, the same his once father used when a rube started kicking tires on the lot. "Good t'see you. Hey there."

The adults flinched at the sound of his voice; the children leaned into it with milky intent.

"We were comin' down the Way and decided to stop a spell, um, maybe see if you had anythin' for barter. Y'know,

tradestuffs. We don't want no trouble. Hey'all, how'zit goin'?"

They stopped at the end of the beginning and the beginning of the end of the shanty hole. From the entry of the largest building at the end of the clutch stepped a massive fellow all jelly and big bones fit into patchwork coveralls. Behind him, rag doll twins, boy and girl, shadowed his steps. The girl chewed rhythmically on the ring finger of her right hand; the boy cocked his head from right to left in gnawed sympathy.

The man came to them with bare feet and a rolling, bovine gait, stopping two arm lengths and a blank stare away. Clouded egg white eyes peered from beneath the sagging brim of his brindle grass hat. His cheeks had long ago surrendered their shape and now sagged as jowls around his bristly chin.

Brahn angled half a step to the left as Kinsey said, "You the headman around here?"

After what might have passed for thought, the man nodded. "Yuh."

Kinsey called up his father's best smile. "Then you're just the man we're lookin' for. I'm Kinsey and this is my partner, Brahn." He glanced at the big man, relieved Brahn did not object. "We thought maybe we could sit down at the trade table an' see how we could help each other out, y'know?"

The boy and girl sidled up to either

side of the headman and looked up at him with wide colorless eyes. The jellied fellow looked at each child and then returned his dull attentions to Kinsey. "Cum'on. We gotta soop pot waitin'." With that, he and the children turned their backs on the newcomers and headed up the Way.

Kinsey cut a quick look at Brahn with a cautious smile and a wink before hurrying to fall into step on the headman's right. Now walking on the downwind side, Kinsey caught a whiff of bitter almonds and bay leaves that crept from the man's fleshy folds. "Thanks, um, thanks for the invitation. You folks look pretty settled here. Nice gardens. You, um, you folks growin' carrots? We got a couple trowels for trade. How 'bout screws, you need those?"

Brahn frowned and fell into step behind them.

The largest building was as spare within as without, the packed earth floor uneven and pitted, a long low table and flanking axe-stripped benches the only furnishings save for the fire pit in the center of the room where soop simmered in a blackened kettle.

Brahn accepted a seat at the table by sliding around the edge of the entryway and coming at the bench from an angle that let him sit at a corner and face the back door although it put his back to the front entry. Kinsey shook his head at the fancy footwork and took his place on

the other side of the table where he could see most of the room, including both doors.

Townsfolk filed in behind them. The headman took two bowls from a pile by the fire and dipped them into the kettle. He handed them to the twins who presented one to each man in silence. Kinsey accepted his from the girl with a smile and a "Thanks much."

Brahn nodded to the boy, his silence intact. The rag doll boy plucked at Brahn's sleeve. He gently and firmly brushed the child's hand away.

"He lahks yew," the headman said, taking up his own bowl.

"Good for him," Brahn said.

One at a time, the adults dipped bowls for themselves and settled around the men at the table, the headman on Kinsey's left, a spindle straw woman with lank blue-black hair and the same milky eyes to his right. A baker's dozen of children stood by the kettle in mute observance of the feast.

A thin slick of grease floated on the surface of the watery stew. As there were no spoons, Kinsey picked the cleanest section of the edge he could find and drank from the bowl as the townsfolk did, gulping it down before he could taste . Six gulps and something warm in his stomach later, he set the bowl down and wiped his mouth on his sleeve. "Haven't had somethin' like that in a while," he said with all the sincerity he could muster.

The headman nodded once, slowly. "We dun get many vizters." The other townsfolk drank in silence, chewing now and again.

"I can bet." Brahn took a single sip. He set the bowl down at the edge of the table.

Kinsey glanced at the children. "Um, it's awful good of you t'offer up a meal, but I hope we didn't take their share."

"Nuh. They dun'like soop."

Probably because they'd had it before, Kinsey decided as he dared another mouthful. The grease curdled on his tongue, declaring it one mouthful too many. He set the bowl down and propped his elbows on the table. "Nice place you folks have managed."

"Yuh." Egg white eyes watched, unblinking. "Yew want more soop?"

"I'm good, thanks," Brahn said.

"Yeah. It's hardly good manners to eat everythin' up when you invited us to the table," Kinsey added. "It's 'preciated, though. Saves us from scroungin' for kindlin' t'night, right, Brahn?"

"Something like that, yeah." The big man carefully shifted on the bench until he straddled the end.

Slurps and the clatter of wood on wood kept time in the silence. Kinsey held the sounds at bay as best he could, if only by pretending the gathering had something to add. "I've never been this far North – I suppose you could call it North, huh? – so I don't know much about this stretch of the Way. I mean, most folks try to settle 'cause they want a place to belong and to make a new life, but me, I've never been able to manage it. I don't mind wanderin', though; I talk to people when I can. There's not much news from South of here, y'know, like, further down the Way that way." Kinsey took his bearings and pointed in the direction they had come. "Mainly good folks like you makin' the best of things."

The crowd met the country compliment with silence. The adults finished their meal within mere swallows of one another, stood as one, and filed away from the bench to deposit their bowls on the pile by the fire.

The twinge of unease when Kinsey walked into town now curled stew grease fingers around his gut. "Um, in fact, what can we do to help you folks out? We don't want to take up all of your time." Kinsey felt the table shift and realized he couldn't see Brahn's hands. He rolled his shoulders under cover of a stretch to make sure he could reach his blades. "And I read somewhere there's miles to go before we sleep, right, Brahn?"

The big man's brow twitched with a frown. "Robert Frost."

"That's the guy."

The children moved together to

stand by Kinsey, the adults a loose knot behind them.

"Th'all lahk yew," the headman said. The children agreed with mouthfuls of needle sharp teeth, emaciated goblins with milky mooneyes.

Kinsey swore, kicking back on the bench as the headman wrapped meaty hands around his neck. He took his eyes off the children long enough to draw steel and thrust it upwards under what he hoped was the headman's sternum, then he was on his feet and the shanty hole folk came at them like a ravenous tide.

As the adults went for his head and the children for his knees, Brahn slammed the table to the right and launched himself towards the backdoor.

The headman grabbed the knife in his chest and tried to pull it free. Kinsey threw himself back and rolled to his feet, coming under a man and a woman trying to pin him down for the rag doll girl and her wicked stepmother claws. He kicked the girl in the face just as Brahn's shotgun barked and half of her head sprayed across the massive kettle. The smoldering coals smoked and popped their thanks while two of the children turned on their fallen neighbor with maddened teeth and claws.

The adults' silence was as terrifying as the goblin children that hissed and squealed as they launched themselves at their dinner. One girl managed to catch Kinsey above the kidney and would have found it if not for another shotgun blast. Kinsey grabbed the still squealing thing and flung her at another child who set upon her with ravenous delight.

The shot from the hip cost Brahn the shotgun as another girl latched onto his wrist and a woman with no teeth cracked a bowl over the back of his hand. The gun tumbled out of his grip to the floor. A boy thing with stringy black hair threw himself at the big man's legs, sinking steel sliver teeth into the back of his right knee. Brahn screamed and swore as he lurched forward a step and hacked at the girl on his arm with the machete. She fell back with one blow, but the boy hung on through two, long enough for the woman to try to push Brahn back. Brahn snarled something Kinsey couldn't make out, brought the machete down in an arc across her face and then stumbled over the body a few steps closer to the backdoor.

Someone swept Kinsey's feet out from under him and he twisted away from a man determined to pin him down. Bloody fear gripped his heart as he realized he couldn't reach his knives or the gun and was going to die. "Brahn! The gun! GET THE GUN!"

Brahn turned to look at Kinsey but didn't take the step to reach the shotgun. Kinsey screamed without words as he threw the man off and

64

kneed a child in the face. *I'm gonna die, gonna die, gonna DIE!* "BRAHNGIMEETH'FUGGIN'-"

Silver and red flashed overhead and the child girl monster thing screamed. Another child leapt at her and tore at the sweet upwelling of blood around the machete. Kinsey staggered to his feet and pushed forward to Brahn. The big man grabbed him by the arm and they were out the door and stumbling towards the Way as the scarlet feeding frenzy spiraled out of control.

"Are you outta your mind? I coulda died back there!"

The shanty hole huddled tense miles and hours behind them. Fear and the incredulity of survival had choked the words out of Kinsey as they traveled, but with jerky and berries in his belly those words came back and brought friends, a mob of friends with spiked chains and ice picks.

Brahn watched the rant from the other side of the fire. "I tried to tell you towns are complicated."

"So that means you stand there with your finger up your butt while those things tear my face off?" Kinsey could hear the squeals of the goblin children in the fire, feel the starving silence of the adults pressing in around him, the sing-song *fresh meat, fresh meat,* that made no sound. And when one of their own bled, the others were so hungry...

"I said I was sorry. You want me to say it again? Fine. I'm sorry."

"Sorry! Oh, yeah, that's rich. Kiss my ass an' make it feel better, why don'cha?" Kinsey threw up his hands to keep them from shaking. "I lost two of my knives back there, y'know. Those aren't easy to come by." Memories of needle teeth and milky eyes hung in the dark when he blinked; they would always be there, ready to tear through his clothes to get at the meaty bits. He clutched at the white-hot anger for as long as he could to hold the worst of the fear at bay. "I thought we were partners, huh? I got your back, you got mine. All you had to do was get the gun, or kick it to -"

Anger knotted along the big man's jaw. "We made it out. Drop it, okay?"

"- me, or even pull 'em offa me, but you stand there –"

"I couldn't reach it, awright?!"

"- like you're so much macho. What the hell you couldn't reach it? One step, mebbe two, you kick it to me –"

Brahn threw his cup into the fire amidst a shower of blue sparks. "Because I couldn't move!"

Kinsey threw his as an encore. "Wha'th'hell is that supposed t'mean?!"

"It means I couldn't move."

The vacant certainty of the admission stripped away Kinsey's fear. He'd heard that same tone as he stood

65

with his grandfather at his grandmother's grave, words burdened with the failure to accept those things that could not be changed despite the wisdom to know the difference. "Huh?"

Brahn dropped his head in his hands and sat in silence. Not knowing what else to do, Kinsey eventually fished the tin cups out of the fire with a twig and set them to the side before herding stray coals back inside the fire ring. He glanced at his partner now and again, his pulse not quite as loud in his ears.

"I can't go back the way I came," Brahn said finally in the same flat tone.

"Um. . ."

"I can't walk backwards."

"Then turn around an' walk forwards." It was the answer of the moment and seemed reasonable enough to Kinsey.

"Gee, why didn't I think of that before? Thanks for the tip, Einstein."

The hollow sarcasm stung the remains of Kinsey's pride after his rant. "I was only tryin' t'help."

Barbed seconds settled between them until Brahn hunched his shoulders in what might have been a shrug. "Yeah. . .Yeah, I guess you were," the big man said.

"So, um. . ." Kinsey fussed with the fire as he tried to find something meaningful to say and was forced to settle on the truth. "I don't understand."

Brahn rubbed his face with both hands. "Yeah, well, that makes two of us." He considered the fire and things Kinsey could not see. "There's a lot of things that don't make sense in this place. Well, some things do." His expression caught the memory of something dark and settled around it in unforgiving lines.

"I mean, really, I don't get it. How can you not walk back where you were?"

Brahn dragged his attention away from the flames. "Just like I said. I can't do it."

Kinsey had never been very good at math as a child, hell, even as an adult, but two plus two did not equal five. "It's not like a choice thing, is it?"

"No."

"You, um, you didn't have this problem before, y'know, back when the world was normal, did you?"

Brahn stared at him in silence.

"Okay, I thought I'd ask is all," Kinsey held up the smoldering twig in a ceasefire. "I mean, I was the one they were settin' to eat, remember?" Kinsey knew it was the wrong thing to say the moment the thought came into his head and leapt out of his mouth. "Right, towns are complicated. Never mind."

There was night, and fire. In the distance, a rippled howl sent up uneven strands of iridescent silver along the southern reaches. Kinsey thought of

66

needle teeth and his grandmother's grave. "What about, um, like, running back?"

"Tried it," Brahn said in resigned anticipation.

"Crawling?"

"And hopping, and rolling, and skipping, and, and, and. If you can think of it, then I've tried it, and probably even a few ways you wouldn't consider. Look. . ." Brahn regarded Kinsey in the dim teal light, his nose a mass of gristle that overshadowed his face. "Let me ask you something. How'd we get back to the Way?"

"We ran our butts off," Kinsey said.

"No, how exactly did we do it?"

"Um, you grabbed me, we headed out the back door, an' we ran." *And I didn't piss myself because I didn't want those kids to smell it and come after us.*

"C'mon, Kinsey, think about it. How exactly did we get back to the Way?"

Kinsey didn't want to think about it, but the pointed insistence demanded he did. He remembered against the backdrop of the fire because it was safer than the dark of closed eyes. "Okay, um, you got my arm and we made it out the door. You were limpin' pretty bad."

"Yeah, but what direction did we go out the door? It wasn't straight out."

Kinsey nodded as he rewound the memory for closer consideration. "No, you're right, you're right. You scraped along the left side of the doorway pretty tight an' then you went off at a left angle three, maybe five, steps, then cut left again but not so sharp that time."

Brahn nodded. "Obtuse angle."

"Yeah, whatever." Kinsey watched their escape play out once more, the Spielberg of his own imagination as he tried to catch it from as many perspectives as possible. Survival didn't always allow for thought; hindsight filled in the blanks. Kinsey locked eyes with the big man over the fire. "We coulda run straight to the Way after we got out the door an' made that first left, but we didn't."

Brahn nodded. "I noticed you looked at me when I walked into the building. Make sense now?"

Even with the wonders and horrors he'd seen since waking up under a pink sky, what the big man suggested seemed a bit farfetched. "I mean, if you can't walk backwards or whatever, how come we couldn't've just turned left an' run straight?"

"You'll be the second to know as soon as I figure that out," Brahn said, getting to his feet. "All I know is that I can't." He brushed the dirt off his backside, closed his eyes for a moment, and then turned his back on Kinsey. He took ten slow steps away from the fire. A shadow of his former self at the edge of the firelight, he turned around and said, "Get my cup and come around the other side." Kinsey did. "Now throw the

67

cup in front of you, not so close I can reach if I stand where I am."

Kinsey did that as well. "Okay, what next?"

Brahn took a deep breath and tried to take a step towards the cup. He failed. Kinsey watched him strain, his legs tighten, his arms move in the barest sympathy of an arc as the big man's weight attempted to shift for a first step. Brahn grimaced, his head craned forward, demanding in vain that the body follow. He relaxed a bare second and then his hands balled into fists as he tried to throw his body at the cup. He crouched to jump, leapt up, and came not an inch closer. A step to the left, and Brahn challenged both trying to reach the cup and taking a mirror step to the right, to no avail. The same result was had when he turned away and attempted to walk backwards, or drop to the ground to roll, or any of a number of other options. Kipping up in a handstand, impressive for a man his size, proved as futile an attempt as the rest.

Kinsey watched as Brahn attacked the desire to retrace his steps only to be shot down by the impossible. The acrobatic routine would have been comical if not for the smooth desperation and futility of repetition. Brahn was now ten steps further along in life; there was no going back. Kinsey heard the cynicism and pain at the core

68

of that fact when Brahn said, "Can you get my rucksack? I can't reach it from here."

Kinsey was too stunned to do anything else. "Wow. I mean, you weren't kidding!"

"Nope."

"Is it always like that?"

"Yup." Brahn settled to the ground and folded his coat as a pillow before stretching out. As he stared at the starless sky, his fingers found their way under his worn leather belt.

"There wasn't even anythin' like a force field like the ones on teevee, well, y'know, when we had teevee. Your clothes never looked flat or anythin'. I mean. . .wow, I can't imagine what that's gotta be-"

"Can we talk about something else?" Bone weary need leeched any anger from the words.

"Oh. . .oh! Yeah, sure thing. Um, lemme get our stuff." He thought of tossing Brahn his gear, escaping into the night. No. Partners didn't play dirty. If Kinsey didn't want to be alone at that moment, he couldn't believe Brahn did either.

They settled on the far side of the fire. Kinsey fidgeted with his gear, unpacking and repacking his knapsack, going through his pockets, checking his remaining blades. He tucked one under the knapsack cum pillow and another under the brush within easy reach by his head.

Kinsey might have envied Brahn his calm as the big man lay there so still, but that was about all. He gaped at abandoned thoughts like *does it hurt to not move like that?*, and *what happens if he forgets something?*, and *I'm glad that's not me.* They weren't safe thoughts, Kinsey was sure.

Camped for the night on the dusty shoulder of an alien Way with a man with a secret, he could think of only one thing to do. "That stew was pretty gross, huh?"

Brahn pursed his lips as if tempting a dry smile that preferred its own company. "Yeah."

"I mean, how was I to know they couldn't cook. I've never been this far up the Way."

"Funny that; neither have I."

"Yeah, um, I guess not."

Brahn crossed his feet at the ankles, his stacked boots a mountain in miniature in the firelight. "How's about next time I chose where we eat, 'kay?"

"Sure thing. Um. . .How's your leg?"

"Stiff. You did a good job with needle, partner."

Kinsey watched his dim shadow ripple over Brahn in the greater dark. The big man continued to stare at the sky. "You're welcome."

Days and miles later, Kinsey thought about how way led onto way. It could have been Frost, or maybe Poe or Twain, or any of the other writers Kinsey had ignored in high school who said it first; he didn't think it was his own idea. Maybe the writer meant to say "how way leads on to Way", but thoughts like that made Kinsey realize he didn't know the questions let alone the answers.

They'd left the rolling orange grasslands and shanty holes behind; now the Way followed the path of greatest resistance up the side of an old man mountain with a massive granite nose and shale cheeks cut deep with thoughtful age. Brahn kept to the Way, so Kinsey did as well even though he would have preferred an easier route. Loneliness had its own agenda.

They clambered over rocks the slumbering girth of bull elephants, and left behind thirty-two carefully hoarded feet of Kinsey's hemp rope when they reached a ledge where a murder of wild roses nested their brood. A day later, a tumbled slide down the far side of the peak smoothed into scholarly foothills with beards of chartreuse and plaid lichens. Kinsey thought they looked like poets and made as much sense.

Brahn said little as they walked, so Kinsey filled the silence. He talked about growing up in St. Paul: preferring impromptu stickball with his friends to parent-sponsored leagues; cannonballs off the deep end of the pool at the Y. He spoke at length of the village of three-armed, bearded women he'd passed through during his first week of wandering, and of the talking pigs with opposable thumbs and cleavers that chased him off the Way and into fluorescent green swamps, razorbacks chanting "St. Louis!" and "The other white meat!". Brahn nodded in all the right places, rolled his eyes in many of the others, and kept moving forward.

"Not that I woulda minded goin' all the way, y'understand," Kinsey said one afternoon as a chevron of geese flew backwards across the sky, "but Buck an' his girl – what was her name?. . .Sarah!, right, right – Buck an' Sarah were in the front seat an' Paulette was shy that way. Besides, her dad was a minister."

"Lucky for her," Brahn said.

Kinsey wasn't certain how to take that, so he left it. "It sucked, y'know, well, because she, um, she didn't, but we had a good time watchin' the movie, an' on the way home - Hey, you got smokes!"

Brahn tapped a cigarette from the red and white box and set it between his lips. "Yup," he said around the filter.

"Where'd you get'em?"

Brahn reached into his coat and pulled out a slender box of wooden safety matches. "Same place I got these. My pocket."

70

"Your pocket? You've had them all this time and didn't tell me?"

"Nope, just found 'em."

"All I ever find in my pockets are crumbs and lint."

Brahn shrugged and tipped a match out of the box.

As he watched Brahn drag the red and white match head along the strike strip, Kinsey rubbed his mouth with the back of one hand. A wisp of flame sparked to life with a hint of sulfur. Brahn held the match to the fertile promise of the cigarette's tip.

"I didn't know you had cigarettes. Marlboro, huh? Can I, um, bum one off ya?" Kinsey couldn't be certain by the look of it, but the first whiff of smoke left him hoping it was a full pack.

Brahn nodded and tapped out a second, squinting through the smoke. "It's your coffin."

Fumbling fingers nearly dropped the cigarette in anticipation, but Kinsey managed to bring it to his mouth and accept a light. The first drag was as smooth as 40-grit white lightning and sweet as salt in a wound. Kinsey staggered to a stop. He hacked up something foul as his stomach threatened to leap out of his mouth and slap the cigarette from his hand.

Brahn paused and watched Kinsey with a wry smile. Smoke curled from his nose. "You okay?"

"Yeah, yeah. . .fine," Kinsey said,

wiping the tears from his eyes. He took another drag, drawing the smoke and memories deep into his lungs. He couldn't recall the last time he needed to shave, but he remembered his final cigarette the morning before the world changed. Memories like that were forever. "Wow. . .that's good."

"I can tell." Brahn continued walking, leaving ash in the wake of his past.

Kinsey caught up a few steps and two drags later. The twitch and rush of the smoker's high had settled in, coaxing his stomach back into his gut with promises of one cigarette, that's it, no more, well, maybe one more, but it's not that bad now, right? His stomach hedged its bets, an occasional twinge serving as a reminder of its dissatisfaction.

He savored the last drag until the filter threatened to melt; only then could Kinsey bring himself to drop it on the Way and grind it under his foot. He was about to ask for another one when he realized Brahn was not even half way through his own smoke. The mauve tip flared and dimmed with every agonizingly slow drag, taunting Kinsey's nic fiend.

Brahn's deliberate absence of expression said he was thinking about things Kinsey didn't need to know. Kinsey asked anyway rather than bogart another smoke. "So, you just find cigarettes in your pocket, huh?"

Brahn didn't look at him, nor did he look away. For Brahn, there was only the too far horizon. "Yup."

"What brand do you smoke?"

"Doesn't matter. These are Marlboros. I've had Pall Malls, too. Kools once."

"This is like your walking thing, isn't it?"

Brahn gave a curt nod that jerked the smoke chain down in a frayed strand.

"You ever find anythin' else in your pockets?"

"Nope."

"Oh. Well, I mean, stuff that would be useful, yeah? You could fish through your pockets an' find just about anythin', y'know? I mean, like, maybe bullets or cartridges, or food, stuff like that. Is it only that pocket, like your pocket wants cigarettes an' they're there, or-"

"Kinsey?"

"Yeah? Right. . .never mind." Kinsey managed to hold his curiosity at bay until Brahn finished his cigarette; no easy feat when he wanted a smoke and an answer. "So, um, what's so special about cigarettes?"

Brahn dropped the butt and snuffed it with a quick twist of a boot. "I only smoke when I'm thinking."

"You think all th'time."

"Sometimes."

Kinsey nodded to pretend he understood. "Did'ja smoke before all this happened?"

Silence. Under the mop of shaggy curls, Brahn's ash eyes considered the Way ahead as if searching for a loose thread to unravel its tapestry. Kinsey hated this part; it meant keeping to himself as they walked. Brahn talked on his own time or not at all.

Kinsey was down to eighty-eight bottles of beer on the wall when Brahn said, "I think I caused everything to happen."

"Sure thing." Kinsey laughed until he realized Brahn wasn't. The unflinching remorse in the big man's profile killed any humor in the moment. Kinsey pressed his lips together, swallowed, and tried again. "I don't get it."

Brahn shrugged. "It's the truth as far as I can tell."

"That's dumb. I mean, it's not dumb like you're dumb, but you can't say it's the truth because you think it is. That's like my sayin' it's all my fault 'cause I think it's all my fault. You know what I mean, anyway. It just doesn't work that way."

Brahn slipped another cigarette out of the pack for himself and then one for Kinsey who tried not to take it too quickly. They shared a match and the crunch of one foot in front of another, Kinsey puffing nervously while Brahn filled his steps with slow drags and soft ribbons of smoke.

"Does it?" Kinsey said as the smoke soured on his tongue.

72

"That's the problem. I don't know," Brahn said carefully. "You said it yourself. How many normal people have you seen except me? People aren't people anymore. Until I came across you, I thought I was the only one left." Brahn took a final drag and flicked the butt into the rocks off the Way. "I can't go back. . .walk back. That's how I lived my life before everything changed, always on the move even if I never went anywhere." Loneliness and dark things caught the corners of the big man's mouth and dragged them down. "I've walked away from a lot of things in my time. People, too." The last words hid themselves in the rustle of Brahn's coat.

Kinsey had been taught to count to ten if he didn't know what to say. He made it to seven. "Okay. Um. . .wow. I mean, it just. It still, it still doesn't make sense, though. I mean, what makes you think it's your fault just because. . .well, just because?"

Brahn hitched his rucksack higher on his shoulder. "A feeling, that's all. Like knowing you'll die if you stop breathing."

Kinsey hated that sort of logic. "That's messed up."

"Something like that, yeah." Brahn picked a piece of tobacco off his tongue and flicked it to the side. "There was a man two days before I met up with you. He had no eyes and was covered with shaggy blonde fur, something like an afghan hound. He was digging a hole on the side of the Way with a slab of blue stone." A third cigarette was called to serve. "I recognized him."

"You did, huh?"

The big man nodded; the cigarette bobbed an absent backbeat between his lips. "My father called him Uncle Henny, a friend of the family – worked in real estate, I think. He would spend the holidays with us. My sister and I adored him when we were kids. He was a nice guy, except when he drank scotch."

Kinsey stuffed his hands in his pockets. "Did you say anythin' to him?"

Brahn's lips clenched tight around the filter, a tense contrast to his otherwise placid expression. "There wasn't anything left to say."

It was easier to believe in Santa Claus than to accept what he'd been told, but Brahn walked beside him and Kinsey hadn't seen hide nor hair of Santa since well before puberty. Still, he took one final stab at making sense of it all. "That could have been anyone, maybe even no one since nothin' says the folks here are all people from back home."

"You still breathin'?" Brahn said around his smoke.

Kinsey winced. "Yeah." Silence stacked questions and knocked them down again, but it was selfish and didn't share any answers.

"So, she has this third eye right here, right?,-" Kinsey pressed his index finger to the center of his upper lip. "-an' every time she smiles it squints at me. The thing is so bloodshot you would think it went on an all-nighter an' left her behind because both her other eyes look fine."

"Up where they belonged?" Brahn said as he continued to examine the blue wooden rifle in his lap.

"Well, yeah, I mean, they were eyes after all."

"Right."

"The place wasn't very big." Kinsey paced slowly around the center of the copse of purple trees. "Six huts and the berry tree orchard. No one else came out to talk, but I could see 'em watchin' me from behind the curtains." He had gone ahead earlier that day to scout out the fruit stand and town in question before he and Brahn parted company, Kinsey to barter for fresh berries and half a wheel of cheese, Brahn to sit tight where he could work on the new rifle undisturbed while still within earshot if his partner called for help.

"Mmm." The big man picked up the gourd beside him and slid it along the barrel until it settled into place with a soft pop. "That should do it."

"You finally got it to work?" Kinsey took a closer look at the gun, a slender hollow branch of a barrel with a black and yellow gourd that did double duty as butt and clip.

Brahn stood, taking up the rifle and his rucksack. "Pretty much. I think those pellets are seeds and they feed through the barrel back here. There's some sort of chemical reaction when you press the trigger pad; it almost smells like burnt toast when you fire off a shot." He nodded in the direction of a tree sporting a splintered hole in the middle of the trunk. "We have maybe five pellets left. The guy must not have had time to fire it."

They'd salvaged the odd-looking rifle and a handful of other needful things three days ago from the rider of a massive opalescent beast more rhinoceros than elephant. Neither the beast nor rider were in any condition to protest the salvage effort. "That's not bad. It looks like the shot went in, um, maybe two inches."

Brahn secured the rifle through two canvas loops on the side of the rucksack. "About that."

"That'll come in ha – whoa!" The ground dropped out from under Kinsey and then slammed back hard enough to rattle his teeth. His knees buckled as he grabbed a branch and waited for the tremor to pass. "Dammit, I hate those things."

"I never noticed." Brahn gathered his scant handful of simple tools and dropped them in one of the many pockets of his duster.

The first tremor ten days ago had knocked Kinsey into the bushes, leaving him leery of the traitorous ground. As far as Kinsey was concerned, the ground wasn't supposed to move. St. Paul wasn't big on earthquakes; blizzards, yes, earthquakes, not so much. Brahn merely brushed off the dust and kept going, or, as Kinsey said after the third tremor in two days, Brahn "took them in stride". The big man had rolled his eyes and kept moving.

Now Kinsey followed in the wanderer's wake as Brahn threaded his steps through the trees and back to the Way a comfortable distance past the town. "The fruit girl said something about tremors when I asked about them," Kinsey said. "She said somethin' about manaques, too, at least I think she did. I couldn't always understand her."

The suns high in the clear pink sky promised a handful of good walking hours. A scatter of low hills masquerading as mountains remained a constant against the impossible horizon, a tantalizing and measurable goal if nothing else. Kinsey danced an occasional jig as they wandered along languid curves through a scattering of pools of brown goo. "Y'know, I've been thinkin' about what you said some time back, about all this being your fault an' all –"

74

"Mmmmm." Brahn did not dance even once.

" – an' it got me to thinkin' about something." He waited for an encouraging word that didn't come. "Why am I here?"

Brahn sniffed softly, a muted basso sound from his misshapen nose. "Because, remember, no matter where you go, there you are."

"What?"

"Never mind."

"No, seriously. Why am I here? Why me? I mean, think about it, you said yourself that folks aren't like they used to be, right?, and that I was the first person lookin' person you'd ever seen since the change."

"Okay."

"That's just it," Kinsey said, warming to the subject. He picked up stray pebbles and skipped them down the dusty Way as they walked. "What am I doing here? I mean, if all this is your fault – an I'm not sayin' it is or isn't, because I don't know enough about anything to say one way or another, y'know? – then how come I still look like me an' we met up? Maybe I'm someone special. Maybe we met up for a reason."

"Sorry, can't help you there."

"Yeah, I know I never saw you before- " At least Kinsey thought that was the case; he was certain he would have remembered Brahn's nose if nothing else. "-but that may not be it. There's all kinda things it could be. Maybe I'm your sidekick, hmmm? Heroes always have sidekicks. Or, how about that I'm your conscience, Jiminy Cricket to your Pinocchio? How 'bout, how 'bout if you're God and just don't remember, hmm?"

"Oh, please."

"I mean it. Stuff like that happens in stories alla time."

"I thought you didn't like reading."

"I don't, I didn't, but I watched teevee so that counts, right? Think about it. I could be anything, the bad guy, the man on the street. Maybe I'm the comic relief."

"Maybe you should shut the hell up," Brahn said dryly.

"I'm just sayin', that's all."

"You never do anything else."

Kinsey recognized the tone and kept to himself after that. He knew he'd struck a nerve when Brahn fished a pack of Camels out of his coat. He was so caught up in shaking theories like Christmas presents that he almost missed Brahn's offer of a smoke and a light. Almost, but not quite.

Despite distance and hope, the tremors did not stop. After one fierce buck and tumble that left Kinsey flat on his back while Brahn waited it out nonplussed, Kinsey could have wished their positions were reversed until he recalled how much he appreciated walking back and forth as he pleased. He settled for picking himself up, shaking out the aches, and moving on. They talked of earthquakes, weather, sports and fresh food; not word one was mentioned about sidekicks, clowns, or other brightly wrapped theories.

A day into the hills, five days out from the orchard town, Brahn's head jerked up and he grabbed the blue rifle. "Incoming!"

Manques leapt down from the cliffs on the left with arms spread wide, using their arm flaps to slow their fall. As one tried to rake him across the face, Kinsey skipped back and drove a fist into its sunken chest. Ribs snapped and he felt the sharp bite of breaking bone in his little finger. They were surrounded in seconds; his finger would have to wait.

The cliffs on the left and sharp drop on the right defining the narrow arena. Kinsey elbowed two of the man-apes aside as he drew steel, wishing for a sword, an axe, anything with more to offer than knives suddenly too small against a band of eight, possibly more. A hiss and two pops to his right, a whiff of burnt toast in the burlap funk, and one of the manaques squealed as its arm was blown off in two chunks. He heard Brahn curse as three more man-apes tried to wrestle the gun from his hands, bearing him irreplaceable steps down the Way.

Kinsey kept on the balls of his feet, facing the emaciated pack with jabs and low slashes. He tried to keep his back to the cliff wall as he made his way to Brahn, but the manaques kept them apart with a feral divide-and-conquer strategy of quick lunges. Kinsey knifed one low in the back as it bounded over his head to get behind him. The move cost him a split second opening as another one sank its teeth into his upper arm and shook its head back and forth. He screamed and slashed at its face; the man-ape released his arm with a bloody, wrenching howl. Kinsey's hand spasmed and dropped the knife. The blade tumbled over the side, leaving Kinsey to jab his fingers in the manaque's bloody eyes and hope that was enough.

He twisted to avoid the clenching mangled claws all around him. Brahn fired again. Kinsey hoped the shot found its mark. There were more than eight; he didn't give himself time to think about what it could mean.

As one came in low to take Kinsey's feet out from under him, the traitorous ground lurched and dropped away. The seizure scattered the manaques like abandoned marionettes, and sent Kinsey sliding down a slope that hadn't been there seconds before. He caught himself on a jagged outcropping as the range shrieked and writhed in seismic pain. Atlas shrugged, the firmament tumbled on its side, and the hills shattered into pillared islands, spines of some beast born of magma and crust far below. Kinsey screamed and scrambled away from the edge, blotting out the cries of a manaque less fortunate.

The tremor drove the ones near him into a panicked frenzy. He fought four of them off – four, five, too many, he couldn't tell – to get his knees and then one foot under him. The wet burlap stench made every breath a struggle. Kinsey caught a glimpse of Brahn on a narrow peninsula clubbing a monkey face before his own troubles piled on him in screaming fury, driving him back down. He screamed and howled back, finding the frightened strength to throw one over the edge of the island and shatter the face of another with a steel toe to the head.

The pack found the tender spots Kinsey could not protect. Hot pain stripped down the back of one leg; teeth found his broken finger and bit it off. He coughed bubbles and blood. "Gahdammit!" It wasn't enough, it was never enough. Monkey-faced children with needle teeth, manaques with milky eyes, all the same and they would tear him apart and pick their teeth with his bones. "Git off me, you uglee fugs!"

The rifle popped and a manaque staggered back, clutching at the tattered remains of its throat. It tumbled off the edge of the world. Kinsey craned his head around to find Brahn on the wrong side of a chasm too far to jump even if he could retrace his steps. "Hep me!" Kinsey felt the ragged bite of something vital giving way in his chest. The manaques howled as Kinsey spit up blood and bile. "Hep! Bru-ahn!"

"My name. Is Stevens." Defiant words, heartbreaking in their clarity. "Brahn. Stevens." Behind Brahn the tiny spit of land widened into the Way continuing ever on, his prison, perhaps his biggest fault. As if to throw it, Brahn hefted the rifle and then lowered it to his side. Shoulders slumped, he turned his back on his partner.

Kinsey could not watch his friend leave. A manaque caught him on the side of the head, sending him into a spiral of bloody thoughts like *sorry I couldn't do more for you, Pinocchio,* and *good job on the leg, partner,* and *nice knowing you, Brahn Stevens.* The joke was on Brahn, and Kinsey the punch line. Just his luck to be comic relief when God didn't have a sense of humor.

Well, joke God if he couldn't take a fuck. Kinsey kept fighting, even knowing that whatever happened next was in the past.

A Spectacular Display

by

Beth Cato

Herein, a tale of science and reasons.

The contrail letters of her name filled the big blue dome of the sky. All across the broad lawn, May heard the whispers and sensed the heaviness of gazes turned her way, but kept her eyes affixed upward. Both hands clutched the knob of her parasol in a death grip.

Kendall never behaved in a low key manner. Each of his inventions had debuted in a spectacularly smashing way. At the World's Fair, he had let his automaton wander the crowds dressed as a dapper gentleman. Last year the introduction of his propulsion pack had taken place at this very festival, as families picnicked and the Retired Noble Gentleman's Band played their staid tunes.

"Is he writing what I think he is writing, Ms. Vanguard?" asked Ms. Anglethorpe, her eyes wide beneath a lavender hat overloaded with blooms.

"Your guess is as good as mine," said May. Above, a W and an I had taken form in puffy white letters, even as her own name began to drift on the wind.

"Mr. Brighton is quite the catch," Ms. Anglethorpe murmured. "You are to be commended, my dear lady."

May didn't need to look at Ms. Anglethorpe. She knew the jealousy and anger that would be veiled in those eyes. Indeed, Kendall Brighton had been coveted in all the society circles. His proletariat background and oil-stained hands created a delightful scandal when he first waltzed into the city, but his roguish smile and smooth words soon had the ladies swooning and the gentlemen curious, and Kendall received what he wanted from both: feminine company, and the men's finances to back his ventures.

May did not succumb to raspy whispers and debonair arched eyebrows. Perhaps it was her dogged refusal that roused him so. That, and

"You are a pretty thing. These toys would soil your white gloves and induce headaches as you struggled to comprehend. Come now. Back to the garden with you."

the hefty inheritance from her father's railroad empire.

Her name had almost faded away. "WILL YOU" now filled the heavens.

"Tell me, Ms. Anglethorpe. Have you ever spoken with Mr. Brighton regarding his inventions?" The dryness in her throat threatened to choke her voice.

"Oh, of course not." The other lady tittered behind a gloved hand. "We spoke about more interesting things than that."

The implications there were rather vulgar, but May dismissed the words with a grimace of a smile.

The machinery—the art of it all—had appealed to May. As a girl, she had stayed up late with her father, assisting him in layouts or deciding on which engine modification to adapt to their fleet. Had Mr. Brighton shared the joys of science and discovery, she would have been a most eager participant.

"You could not understand this," he had said instead, his face contorted in disgust when he found her in his workshop. "You are a pretty thing. These toys would soil your white gloves and induce headaches as you struggled to comprehend. Come now. Back to the garden with you."

"Inventions are such fickle things," May said, fanning herself with a hand as she stared at the sky. It was almost time. It had to be. "They do frighten me. Oh!"

The flow of the vaporous letters ceased. Kendall Brighton hovered in space for a moment and then plummeted like a swatted fly. Around the lawn, murmurs turned to screams.

May managed a scream of her own as the body impacted somewhere in the woods beyond the river. Her hand trembled at her mouth. "God help me," she whispered.

"Oh, Ms. Vanguard!" cried Ms. Anglethorpe. Other ladies crowded around, some sobbing as they murmured condolences.

"He died as he would have chosen to die," May said, her voice husky with emotion. "As a showman." Someone would record the statement for the papers.

She pressed a fist against her chest and forced herself to breathe and stay upright. Later, she would pray and atone for her sin. But now, before the vultures of society, she must play the part of the grieving fiancé.

Kendall's plans for the proposal had been obvious for days; his intentions with her father's estate even more so. When she had confronted him, his smooth façade had revealed the true man beneath.

"You will marry me, Ms. Vanguard," he had said in those slick tones. "I have a barrister willing to produce papers, you see. Papers that bear witness testimony that you and your father were unusually, inappropriately close, and that the reason you remain unwed at thirty is because—

"That is a lie, Mr. Brighton, as you well know."

He smiled then, in that charming way. "Who will be believed, my lovely lady?" His fingers toyed with the lace at her wrist.

May had heard the cruel whispers when she was a child. That she was too important to her father, that she was always underfoot at his offices, that her interests were vulgar and masculine. It would take so little to rekindle the old gossip and twist it into something nefarious.

And Kendall Brighton thought her a fool who would bow to his whim, just as everyone else had.

She took one final look at the sky, where "MARRY ME" stood bold for all the city to see.

The schematics in the workshop had been easy to read. In mere minutes, she had siphoned half of the fuel from his propulsion tank and adjusted the meter to show it as full.

"And the saddest thing of all," she said to Mrs. Anglethorpe, "was he went through all the trouble to ask, and he knew exactly what the answer of my heart would be."

"Oh, my dear lady." Gloved hands squeezed her arm and helped to hold her upright as she worked through the crowd and away from Kendall Brighton's final spectacular display.

PAPAVERIA PRESS

WWW.PAPAVERIA.COM

Specialising in limited, handbound editions and the occasional trade paperback, Papaveria is an independent micro-press publishing poetry and prose in the fields of fairy tales, fantasies and myth.

Books are small gods.

In Defiance of Sleek-Armed Androids
by
Lisa M. Bradley

One day we'll have sleek-armed androids
to hug us like lovers but
I'll still reach for you
because I am broken
like you.
We are reciprocal shards
snapped along matching fault lines:
my chipped edges hook
in your crevices,
your splintered angles graze and snag
my gouges.
The longer we grind together,
the safer our jagged silhouettes grow
for programmed caresses,
fingers calibrated to acceptance.
But in the dark
our crevasses yawn,
ache for shorn and crumbling cleavages
that disgust less-damaged companions,
upset the wholesome parameters
set by quality control.
Perfection is frictionless--
I need to stub my soul on yours,
I need to lick the slivers in your wounds.
I need to pierce myself
on the one
perfectly fractured
other.

(after Jaswinder Bolina's poem "One Day, Androids Will Have Pudgy Arms and Hug
Us Like Mother, But Still I'd Reach for You, Dear Reader, Which Is Why I Have So
Much Faith in Us as a People")

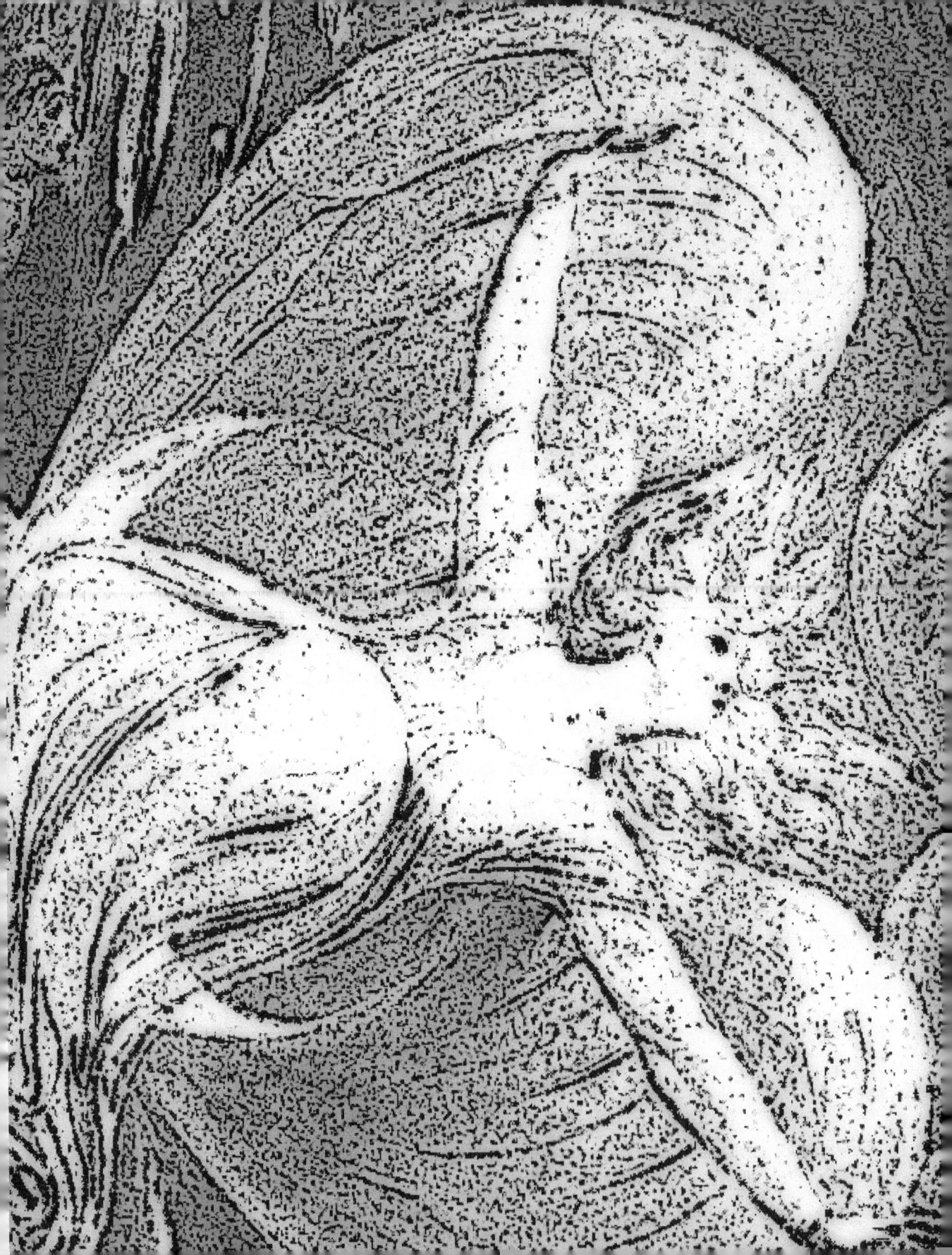

The Lesson of
the Phoenix

by
Julia Rios

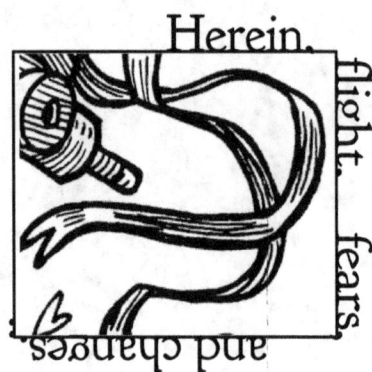

Herein, flight, fears and changes

"Twenty-two." I didn't look up.

Then he asked me over for a playdate, but his mother told him to let me get back to work. Amir didn't give up, though.

"Will you imagine it?" he asked. "Will you dream of it?"

"Sure," I said.

That's how it started.

—

It's always the same in the dream. We're in Amir's back yard, except the yard ends abruptly in a cliff; grass and sod hang over the loose lip of earth, crumbling away as we run close. We're chasing the bird.

—

I was studying at The Phoenix when I met Amir.

"I like your pink hair," he said.

"Thanks," I said. I didn't mean to look up, but the next thing I knew, my work was sitting untouched next to my lukewarm lentil soup, and Amir was telling me all about his bird.

"It's a special bird," he said, flapping one plastic wing. "See how the colors move when it flies? It will chase all the mosquitoes away. They love me, but they will hate this bird."

"Cool," I said, but I tapped my pencil against my stats book as I spoke.

"How old are you?" Amir asked. "I'm seven."

88

I used to dream of you. I'd dream of laughing with you, or curling up next to you, maybe biting your neck just a little. I would dream profound conversations that made sense in sleep, only to come out as garbled nonsense later.

Sometimes I told you the dreams, but only the ones that didn't show me as vulnerable and eager as I truly was. The most you ever said was, "I hardly ever remember my dreams." I wonder if that's true.

Amir is dreaming me now, and he holds on so tightly, it's impossible to go anywhere else.

—

The lesson of the phoenix is that you've got to let go, whether you want to or not.

—

You have to let me go, Amir.

I don't want you to go.

But I bring the monsters with me. As long as I am here, the monsters will come. They will chase you. They may eat you.

My bird will protect me.

He clutches the film of the bird's wings, smearing them with sweaty fingerprints. This bird is not a magic bird. It will not protect Amir from anything. It won't protect me either.

When I used to dream of you, sometimes we were also running from monsters, but I didn't know that they were mine, and that you weren't. I'd take your hand, and we'd flee together, or we'd face the monsters as a strong team. Sometimes there would be kissing, too. I always liked the kissing.

Now there is no kissing, and no strong team. There is just a little boy and a fake bird with a rubberband one might pull taut and release to simulate the launch into flight.

And the monsters are gaining on us.

—

You're still around in waking life. Mostly on the internet. You post a status update, or you show up as one of the addressees in a group e-mail. I suppose this means you must exist. I didn't simply dream you up. But I might as well have. It would in some way be kinder if that were the case. I could pretend you would want me then. If you were real.

—

Other people want me. It's not like I don't have friends.

That's how nightmares work. You bring everything with you and then it materializes bigger and badder than you might have thought possible.

—

Amir wants me.

—

We're in a cave, but it isn't a cave, It's a crawl space under Amir's back porch. The bird has landed there, and we must rescue it. One of its wings is torn, but it is still capable of flying. Amir hands me a roll of tape.

Can you fix it, Geli?

No, I don't fix things. I break them.

I don't believe you.

89

You are destined for disappointment.

He is, too. I should know. You can't have such faith without it leading to disappointment. Still, here I am, rescuing a plastic bird.

——

I have to let you go.

——

You were there last night on the edge of the cliff with me and Amir. You looked so beautiful, your profile to me as I raced to retrieve that silly plastic bird before it went over and away forever. You didn't turn to face me. You stood half immersed in shadow, and said, "It is wrong of you to call me here, Evangeline."

You jumped without a gasp or a scream, just a slight creak of your knees as you pushed off, your long red braid rippling in the sunset.

Then the spiders came racing across the lawn, and I had to stop looking.

——

The lesson of the phoenix is that you have to deal with whatever's in front of you.

——

This reaction I have to spiders is involuntary. I never chose it. I never thought, gee, when I see spiders,

90

how about breaking out all over in goosebumps? No. And it doesn't matter if they're poisonous or not. It's just the way they move, the way their legs look, the essence of spiderdom.

That said, these spiders are poisonous.

And huge.

That's how nightmares work. You bring everything with you and then it materializes bigger and badder than you might have thought possible.

——

Here is no longer a cliffside or a backyard. Here is a cave like in the beginning of *Indiana Jones*. Here is dark and close and full of giant fucking spiders. They can run faster than lightning. They want nothing more than to catch and eat us. Slowly.

So, really, I've got to stop dwelling on you. If there's a right time for that, it isn't now.

Amir takes my hand. His is small and brown and perpetually scabby from some playground game that involves bullies flicking open the skin of the weaker kids' knuckles. Amir doesn't want to play it, but he's not one of the bullies, so he has to anyway. I've never asked why he doesn't go to his mother for help, though she seemed nice enough at the coffee shop. You can't trust adults with stuff like that. They only make things worse.

Today there is also a bruise on his forearm, and another up past the elbow. I frown, but Amir tugs me forward.

We have to fly.

We can't.

The bird will help us. Close your eyes.

I start to argue, but think better of it, and close my eyes obediently.

Run!

I stumble forward, two steps, three, and then my legs are beating at empty air. We're flying.

—

The lesson of the phoenix is that it is impossible to tell on first glance whether something is worthless and weak or majestic and strong.

—

I've flown in dreams off and on all my life, but I never believe I can until it happens.

When it's just me, I always feel like I have to keep in constant motion or else I'll fall. This time I've got a skinny little kid and a plastic bird with me, and I realize as we clear the mouth of the cave, that I am the only one thrashing through the sky.

Amir is still, focused, directing his whole body toward his outstretched arms with intense concentration. The bird is what it always is: plastic. But for the rustle of its taped up wings against the night wind, it's still and silent, too.

How can we be doing this?

Because we have to. If we don't, the spiders will catch us, and that's not how it works. The monsters don't win.

We are over a giant sea now, and the spiders are far behind us. Our altitude has stayed constant as a passenger jet, so I look over at Amir and his sad little bird, and again I notice those hideous bruises all up and down his arms. Both arms.

Where did you get those?

Amir shrugs, a small ripple of the shoulders that I feel where our hands meet.

B B Britches.

What?

It's another game. You have to say B B Britches whenever you say a B word or else they punch you.

Ow. So, I guess you forget a lot?

Amir doesn't look at me. His voice, when it comes, is barely audible.

Sometimes they punch you anyway. Sometimes they punch you even if you don't use any B words at all.

—

I met you at The Phoenix, too. That's why I kept going back in the first place. Their soup isn't really very good, and their coffee's worse. But you might turn up again. And even if you didn't talk to me, maybe you'd notice me, and my pink hair, and my coolness in the face of adversity.

You'd see how over you I was, and then maybe you'd realize your mistake.

—

The lesson of the phoenix is that the monsters only win if you let them.

—

I've been puzzling out these lessons ever since you walked out on me. I brought you flowers that last day. I thought you'd like them, but instead you flipped out. Called me a stalker, and a lot of other things, too.

"You haven't learned the lesson of the phoenix," you said. And you stood. And you turned away.

"Your flowers," I said. As if you taking them would somehow fix everything.

"Don't be such a child, Evangline," you said.

I'm not a stalker. Really. It's not like I followed you home or something. I didn't.

—

I'm not allowed to take my bird to school.

It's not really a school sort of toy.

It would protect me there, if I took it. I know it would.

I don't think so.

It protects me here.

That I can't argue with, and honestly, it's not even my business if he thinks a

92

plastic bird will save him from the humiliation and torture of pre-adolescence. But really, it's like the flowers. The ads make out like when you give someone flowers, they melt with love. In real life, it's nothing like that. Not with you and me at least.

I kept the flowers. I put them in a vase on my kitchen counter and watched them wilt a little more each day, thinking maybe somehow I could channel my care for you into them, and that either they'd grow impossibly bright and strong, or that (more likely) my feelings would wither away to nothing with the shrinking petals. It takes a long time for lilies to fade if you cut the stems every day like the florists advise.

—

The lesson of the phoenix is that you can fly long after you might think you couldn't, and furthermore, that you must.

—

We're running again. Monsters are chasing us. Some of them spiders, and some amorphous things that show claws or teeth or slimy dark eyes depending on how you look.

I'm tired.

I'm tired because this is no way to get rest, this relentless running and flying and being called to Amir's side every night. In the waking world, I'm slipping. I have dark circles under my eyes. My roots are showing. At work yesterday Francisco asked if I was on drugs.

I'm not. Unless dreams are drugs. Unless withdrawals from a former lover count. You were affectionate with me once. I didn't make that up.

Stop, turn, dislodge a claw from my pant leg. Run again.

Amir is flagging, too. His black curls hang heavy and limp against his skull, and his gait is dangerously slow.

We've got to do better than this, Amir.

He doesn't look up. His hands crumple the bird's wings as he stumbles forward. And then he falls.

—

I wake up panting and sweaty in the dark of my room. The downstairs neighbors are having a party, and I can hear the muffled hum of voices, feel the persistent thump of the bass from their music.

I have never been so alone in my life.

—

The lesson of the phoenix is that eventually, the monsters will wear you down.

—

I'm not going to pretend I never cried over you. I did. A lot. But I'd thought I was past that stage. You told me everything up front. You gave me all the clues I'd need, the roadmap to our relationship's impending destruction. Personality disorder, Cluster B, Histrionic, Borderline. I knew these things, but they were just words to me, and you were brilliant. You shone so hot and bright that I didn't care about anything else.

I used to dream of your breasts, before I touched them. They were small and pert, like TV breasts. Magazine breasts. They seemed to me like apples, and I would sometimes imagine the crisp sweetness of an apple in my mouth when I saw them.

"This will change everything," you said on the night when I finally got to second base. Bases. Like love and intimacy are games. Like there are winners and losers. Well, maybe there are.

I thought you meant it would make us more serious about being together.

—

The lesson of the phoenix is that love will fuck you up hardcore.

—

The next three nights Amir doesn't call me. I dream alien landscapes, ice caves, deserts, cinematic car chases. I don't dream of you; I don't even try. Not that this helps me in the waking world. There I am still ragged and tired,

93

my eyes bloodshot as if all I do is drink and smoke or something. I don't. I go to school and to work like nothing's changed, because in the waking world nothing has. My girlfriend dumped me over three months ago. If I'm not over it by now, that's pathetic. That's what Francisco thinks. He doesn't say it in so many words, but it's clear enough.

A month ago I didn't care about anything else. I told myself I had to get over you, but secretly I'd been holding onto that heartbreak for all I was worth. Now I've got other things to worry about, and they're creeping in and clouding my focus.

I don't want to worry about Amir. He's just a random kid I met once. He probably just got bored with the same dream, the same chase over and over. He's fine. I repeat these things to myself, but I know in my heart they're not true.

Here's the thing about Amir: I know he wouldn't get bored. You might get bored. You did get bored if what you told me is true. But not Amir. I saw how tired he was, I saw his bruises, and I saw him fall. The only way he wouldn't be with me now is if he couldn't.

—

The lesson of the phoenix is... why the fuck am I even still trying to think up these lessons? It's not like they're going to make you come back.

94

—

Amir's back yard is empty. There is no sunset, not even the moon, just darkness, and the sad rustle of dry leaves. In this dream, autumn is nearly over, and maybe the stars have gone out forever. I go to the crawl space where I am sure I will find a flashlight. I think of it as I go, of the light it will provide, of the way it will lead me to Amir. If I think it hard enough, it will have to be there.

Under the porch there are cobwebs, and they cling to my arms and my hair as I pass. I try not to think of spiders. I don't have time for spiders tonight. Of course that only makes me think them harder.

A giant leg flexes in the corner, and panic rises in my chest. It's thick and shiny, and covered in bristly hairs. There, by one tarsal claw, is the flashlight I've come for. It's old and dusty, but it's my only chance. *Suck it up, Geli.*

My fingers brush the edge of the flashlight tube, but the spider darts its leg forward and tries to spear my hand. I withdraw just in time to avoid being pinned to the ground. The spider hisses and venom drips from the tip of one fang. A drop splatters onto the flashlight, making the plastic sizzle.

I dive forward, remembering my gymnastics training from when I was a little kid. Dive and roll. I manage to bat the flashlight away from the spider with one arm as I make my rough and tumble pass, but a fleck of venom scores my arm. The sound I make is halfway between yelp and choke.

The spider rears in anticipation of a charge. My only shot at survival is to grab the light and get the hell out of the crawl space. The opening is too small for the spider to pass without taking time to finesse it. I bank on that, and never mind the venom as I reach forward. This time I scream, and it seems like it goes on forever, like there is no sound in the world but screaming.

Fuck, this hurts. I'll be lucky to have any skin left on my hand when I get out of this. If I get out of this. I run, scrambling up the steps and into the unnatural calm of the back yard. There is no sound, no crickets, not even the leaves of before. Now it is just the ends of my ragged war holler, and each leaden footfall as I clomp over the grass.

I flick the switch on the flashlight and it blinks feebly, so I thwap it with my other hand, trying to avoid touching the venom soaked bits. The blink wavers and then steadies, resolving into a thin stream of light. Hardly much at all, but it will have to do. Now where to go next? Where is Amir? I hold him in my mind, remembering: bruises, dark curls, those beseeching eyes, the scabs on his knuckles. His little hands so soft and dry, his voice, his hope, his bird.

Of course it's the bird that sticks.

I trip over it on the lawn. If it looked sad before, this is tragic. It's barely recognizable, beak missing, wings mangled and tattered beyond any hope of flight. No amount of tape could fix it now.

I pick it up, trying to cradle it as gently as I can. "Where's Amir?" I ask, and bite my lip as I wait for a reply, or a sign, or something.

—

The bird doesn't say anything. A gust of wind comes up and sweeps it from my hand, and I watch, dumbstruck as fragments of wing and body scatter in all directions.

—

The lesson of the phoenix is that there is always farther to fall.

—

I am standing at the edge of the cliff, and I have no idea where to go. And then the cliff crumbles, and the world shudders and dissolves around me, like water rippling outward from the impact of a stone.

There's a sick rush in my stomach. I am falling.

For a few dizzy seconds, I flail, and then I give up and wait for the thud of

95

death. I wonder why my life has not flashed before my eyes. That's what everyone says happens, but not for me. Instead I am stuck in an interminable nightmare of hyper-awareness.

And then something else happens. Inside my heart, it's as though a key has turned. I remember Amir's outstretched arms, and the way his whole body, his whole being seemed focused on the goal of soaring.

I bend my will and straighten my limbs.

—

The lesson of the phoenix is that letting go is the only way to grow and revive.

—

When I reach the playground, my landing is perfect. I have absolute control of the flight. Amir's tiny form is doubled over on the swings, limp and lifeless.

Amir?

No answer.

Maybe it's because I really don't want to think about the fact that I may be about to touch a dead body, but right now all the anger I've kept back is bubbling up like lava in my chest. How dare you call me childish? You told me secrets. You kissed me. *You.* Kissed *me.* Not the other way around. Do you go around making out with little kids? I

don't think so. That's just bullshit.

And now I'm right up in front of the swing set.

I start by touching his hand. It's cool, but not frozen, not stiff. He doesn't wake up, doesn't respond, and I realize I've been expecting him to smile and start babbling in that way he always does. Had I really thought it would be so easy, that one epiphany would make everything right?

The lesson of the phoenix is birth and rebirth again and again through trials of smoke and ash and fire (or, you know, flying and dark and giant spiders). And you know what? Fuck you. I can damned well keep thinking of my life in terms of that metaphor if I want.

I hold onto the flame of righteous anger as I hug Amir close and start running, gathering speed to take flight.

—

The return journey takes almost no time. I know my will, and in an instant I am there. The spiders are all around us, but I don't care. I force the air to brighten with the rage light that is my sense of injustice. It burns hot magnesium white. It will kill the spiders if it touches them, because I know it, because I made it, because I will it.

The spiders know it, too, but one comes near anyway. It loses three legs before falling in misery, and I am glad.

Amir, the monsters don't win. You told

me, remember? That's not how it works. You can't let them. Not now. Not ever.

Amir shudders, his chest faintly rattling.

—

I imagine the schoolyard bullies advancing relentlessly. I imagine them as giants, threatening to grind his bones for their bread. My light grows brighter.

He looks so small and wasted against the moonlit grass. I remember his hope, his candor. Is the only way to escape monsters to become one yourself? Or to die? It's not fair.

Then I hear music, faint and sweet. As I look up, a feather floats down through my shield, silver and red and orange and pink. It isn't plastic; it is grander than anything I have ever seen. I catch it and clutch it and press it to Amir's chest. And then we are burning. Not the screaming searing pain of burning alive, but the warm tingle of the inevitable, of change.

—

The lesson of the phoenix is that the only way to escape monsters is transcendence.

—

I awake to sunlight slanting in through the curtains, warming my face. I'm not sure how or why, but I know that I've won something. I wash and dress, ready to take on the homework I have neglected these past several days. As I reach for my bag, I notice the scar. It looks like it's been there for years, this ragged pink line across my forearm. But I know it wasn't before last night.

—

The semester's in full swing, and all the retail stores have been doing their quarterly inventories, which means more work than usual. When I am not knee deep in equations or economic theory, I am seeing strings of numbers in my head. 10 boxes of green beans, $1.49 per can, 24 per box. Retail value: $357.60.

I am so busy that even my dreams are just continuations of my waking hours. Francisco says I'm back on my game. He's teasing me again instead of being gentle in that worried-you-might-break way.

I have a three-hour break in between class and work today, so I head down to The Phoenix to study. I haven't been in a while. I'd gotten to a point where I'd rather avoid you. That's stupid, though. I like The Phoenix, bad soup and all. I like the way the cashier always calls me Miss Pink Hair, and the amateur exhibits by local artists. I like the orange walls and the red vinyl booth seats. Just because I met you there, and you left me there, it doesn't mean The

97

Phoenix is yours.

So of course I'm surprised when I walk in and you're there.

—

The Lesson of the phoenix is that if you think you're ready for something, there *will* be a test.

—

I take a table at the back and spread out my books and notes, ready to commit to memory all the stuff about game theory for tomorrow's exam. I don't even look at you. I'm not going to let you think you have any sway over me.

It's twenty minutes before you crack and come over. You can't stand that I'm not desperate to see you.

"Evangeline," you say. Your voice is arch, half bite, half purr. I'd be lying if I said it wasn't still sexy as all get out.

"Brigid," I say. My tone is neutral, maybe edging on wary. I don't look up from my work.

"I'm going by Brigida now," you say.

Of course you are. You need the exotic appeal. You're not getting enough attention.

"Did you want something?" I ask. I look up, keeping my face carefully blank even though my heart is pounding.

"Just to say hi," you say, and you toss your braid over your shoulder so it will ripple and catch the light. That used to

be my undoing, and you know it, but I am not playing this game anymore. You are more trouble than you're worth.

"Hi," I say. And then I point at my work. "I have an exam tomorrow, so I really can't talk right now."

"I won't keep you," you say. Your smile could kill me with its sharpness if I get too close.

"Well, bye then," I say.

You raise your chin, thrusting your shoulders back so that the rhinestones on your shirt jut out and glitter under the fluorescent lights. Lady Killer. Yeah, well, not this lady. I bend my head toward the pages spread out before me.

You don't say goodbye before you flounce away to sit at a table conspicuously within sight of mine.

I try not to indulge the sick part of me that wants to play your game. The part of me that is angry and glad I have you dancing to win my attention. If I give in, you'll only eat me alive all over again.

—

I've lost track of how many coffee top ups I've had by the time I look up again. It's the sweet high voice that does it. "Mama, can we have milkshakes?" Amir.

They walk through the café looking for a good seat, and then he sees me, and the unaffected joy in his face hits me like a blast of lightning.

"Geli!" He breaks free of his mother's grasp and runs over to my table.

"Amir!" His mother calls. "Don't bother that lady."

"It's okay," he says. "She's my friend."

I nod at his mom. "We've met here before. He showed me his bird."

"Oh, that bird," his mother says in the long suffering tone of a parent who has heard of nothing else for ages.

"Can we sit with Geli? Can we?" He asks, bouncing up and down in excitement.

I smile to let his mother know it's okay with me, and she acquiesces.

"If we're bothering you, just let me know," she says as they sit down.

"It's no bother," I say. "I need a study break anyway."

Amir slides in next to me and presses close. I'd forgotten how easily young kids will snuggle. It's actually pretty nice.

"How's school going?" I ask, risking a glance at his arms. They're bruise free.

"I'm friends with Joshua and Daniel," he says. "We eat lunch together."

"That's nice," I say. "No more BB Britches?"

"No," Amir says. "I said it was dumb, and that's when Joshua and Daniel liked me. They think it's dumb, too. My bird says they're good."

"Your bird talks?" I ask.

The milkshake arrives then, and Amir pauses to take a long slurp before he points to his chest. "It doesn't have to talk. It's in my heart."

I flash back to the last dream, and the feather falling. I know that if I were to peel off his sweater and his t-shirt, I'd find a pink, feather-shaped scar on his chest.

As if he knows what I'm thinking, Amir traces my pink forearm scar with one finger. "I like you Geli," he says. "Thank you for being my friend."

I ruffle his hair. "I like you too, Amir."

—

"Evangeline," you say as I pass your table.

I can't help turning to look.

"Still playing with children, are we? I see you never learned the lesson of The Phoenix."

"Are you going to enlighten me?" I ask.

You bare your teeth, and I wait for the inevitable bite. "Chance meetings with strangers in coffee shops don't mean a damned thing."

Your lips press together in a hard line when I laugh.

"Okay, Brigida. Whatever you say." I wave to Amir one last time before I walk out of The Phoenix and into the crisp autumn evening.

Songs for the Devil
and Death
by Hal Duncan.
172 pages.
Paperback.

Reviewed by Alexandra Seidel

"*This is the song of Orpheus, a song unbound by time. / This is the song bound only by the lover's rhythm and the poet's rhyme*" may just be a perfect summary of Hal Duncan's 'Songs for the Devil and Death', but even in the strength of these two brief lines, you can only get a whiff, a glance of the height and depth, of the blackness and the light captured on these pages.

It is hard to recommend the proper setting in which to read this little book of verse and truth, and even so, it feels like it wants and needs a setting. Wine, tissues, or an audience made up of an army of sinners may all work at some point, may all be necessary. That said, some of these poems cut so deep that you may cry or laugh yourself to tears, some of them will want to make you shout what you are reading to the world, which is why reading in public spaces may draw unwanted attention, please be aware of that before you get on the bus.

The collection consists of individual sonnets and of poems grouped under different headings. The individual pieces are chosen to connect the longer works, a structure that presents a flawless whole. In here, only some of the work is given a closer look, those being the songs that spoke to me most.

The Sonnets for Orpheus are perhaps

a little bit my favorites, but never by much. *"I'll sing of the vine, the grain, the salt, and sex. / I'll sing you my soul. I'll open up and bleed. / Muses, as Graces, all I ask--give me the charms I need"* for example resonates with the poet in me, but everyone who has ever contemplated to do anything with passion should be able to relate. These words want to be shouted and sung, like a concert, a mad choir of harpies or furies or...poets: *"he'll break the hearts of weak and strong / and Death himself will sing along. // Here is my Orpheus, his severed head held high, / his tongue as lethal as Medusa's eyes."* Most of all, the Sonnets for Orpheus speak of liberation without pretense, of the human need to break free: *"Now, a new sun rises, proud as the morning glory of a cock. / Now Orpheus sings again, song shattering Prometheus's rock."*

Wake can at the most be whispered in the silence of solitude, the words catching in your mouth as you swallow to keep the tears down. These are deeply personal poems, angry poems, but even so or just because of that I could directly relate to them, the way in which words are so meaningless in grief, the way Christianity is nothing but reviling without the mask of faith. *"As--heaven--is on earth--it is / On coffined love a stranger's piss, // This service prattle preaching zeal, / Magician's dove and Judas kiss[.]"*

Sonnets for Kouroi Old and New is best imbibed in between glasses, in between kisses, cheers and jeers, in between climaxes. They are a sequence of carnal seduction, clearly drawn in he likenesses of the heroes of Greek myth and legend, they are a *"mischief with the mysteries of flesh and the bliss / is clearly woven from silk words to snare more than a kiss."*

Sonnet 29 and Amorica sting and sting again, speak of love and insecurity, of holding on, of giving our selves to love because there is nothing else we can do. *"[A] thousand thorns may drive me wild / and I will bleed for love, and to my death be reconciled."* and the thorns stay, dissolving in your flesh until they run in your blood.

Still Lives is an ossuary, a place brimming with rotten fruit. It touches you because it is so true, and you know it. It clings to you because that is what the smell of rot does. Be afraid, for sometimes *"all the lies are true."*

"We cannot step twice into the same river; / for the waters flow fresh over and they flow forever" are words From the Fragments of Heraklitos, a gathering of poems that I read several times, finding something new in each read. These poems are--like many others, directly or indirectly-- concerned with truth: *"This world, which is the same for all, / no single god or man has made;"* and *"time is a child*

101

playing draughts, / the power of a king in a child's grasp." are some of the things that I found meaningful during my latest read, things that made me think.

And there is of course The Lucifer Cantos, raw and neat and true as all of the above. Hungry. Greedy. If you cannot take the earth, take this instead, or rather, take the earth and fill it with the cards shown here, shuffle well, and deal: *"I do not threaten, do not lie, / but only warn: we will reclaim the sky."*

After finishing the book, I had the slight urge to set fire to something, to sneak into a church and shout obscenities, just to hear the echo of these words in the pews. You know, perhaps operating heavy machinery after reading 'Songs for the Devil and for Death' is not such a good idea. If ever there was a worthy sacrifice to Dionysus and Death, then Reader, it is this book.

The 'Songs for the Devil and Death' are a battle cry, a primal sigh, a guiltless moan, but most of all--most surprisingly of all--they are ruthlessly honest. Quite apart from that, Hal Duncan shows a mastery of language and structure that I find admirable. In conclusion, although this book has certain drug-like qualities, every human being should own a copy. Reader, believe me when I say you want this book.

The Jelly Fish Queen

by

Jaelithe Ingold

Herein... the hell of high school... with fauna.

They call her the Jellyfish Queen.

Even now she stands upon the rocks above the shore. The wind whips around her face and flutters her green jacket. If she were a beautiful girl, it would be worthy of an impressionist painting.

But Cordelia isn't beautiful. She isn't willowy and graceful, nor is she blessed with fine features. She's plain. Her figure is short and plump, and her hair is long, blonde and straggly like jellyfish tentacles.

Cordelia turns and looks down at me. Her shadow stretches on the sand in front of her, but it doesn't quite touch me. Her hand rises in a half-hearted wave, but she isn't smiling. I can't bring myself to smile either.

I hate her even more than I hate jellyfish.

Three weeks earlier

"Did you know there are two body forms for jellyfish? One is called the polyp, and the other is called the medusa?"

I look up from my tattered copy of Wuthering Heights, even though it's the last thing I want to do. Honestly. Why is she nattering on and on about jellyfish when I'm clearly busy?

"Did you know that, Kate?" Cordelia rests her hand on my arm and looks at me with those watery blue eyes. There's a hint of strain in her voice.

I sigh and relent. "Like the Medusa whose gaze turned people to stone?"

A smile flashes across her chubby face. She's grateful for this small bit of attention, although I don't even want to give her that much. She's supposed to be my best friend, but lately, Cordelia has been unbearable.

"Sort of. It's the body type you think about whenever you think 'jellyfish.'" She makes little quote marks with her fingers. "But those aren't snakes arranged around their heads. Jellyfish have tentacles with stinging cells called nematocysts..."

I pretend to listen as she continues listing the characteristics of an animal I care nothing about. Instead, I gaze around the cafeteria and notice how much more interesting the other students seem in comparison. And then there's Jason Crawford.

He's seated with the rest of the swim team. All of them--both the guys and the girls--have broad shoulders and lean forms. Jason isn't the most handsome. Nor is he the best swimmer, the captain or anything else.

I've never spoken to him, but his presence churns my stomach more than the uneaten chicken sandwich in front of me.

Today, the biology classes are taking a field trip to the zoo.

"Let's go to the aquarium." Cordelia moves ahead of me. Why doesn't she ever cut her hair? She's walking faster than usual, but the limp strands barely move against her back.

Of course she's excited. She gets to spend an hour with her jellyfish.

We're studying Animal Behavior, so our teacher wants us to pick an animal and make notes of its activity. We're supposed to count how many times it eats, shits, pisses, sleeps and moves around its enclosure.

I have no desire to spend an hour watching jellyfish float, but I don't know where else to go. Everyone else already seems to have their animals picked out. Most have chosen the monkey house. Doug Bryson claims he's seen the monkeys jerking off.

An opportunity, I suppose, to put that kind of information into a school report without consequences.

But I don't want to go there. Nor do I want to join the group of girls who've chosen the penguins and seals because they're just sooooooo cute.

So I follow Cordelia, because at least it'll be quiet in the aquarium. I'll pick an ordinary fish, spend the hour reading and fudge the numbers.

The aquarium is dark in comparison to the sunny zoo, but the chlorine-scented air is strangely pleasant. Tank after tank is lit to reveal both pretty and ugly fish. The place is soothing and warm and seems like another, shadowy world.

Cordelia finds the jellyfish easily. The seven tanks are lit from below to illuminate the umbrella and tentacles of the blobs. There is something fragile and graceful about them, although I don't really understand the obsession.

As I watch, Cordelia walks to the largest of the tanks. Even though there

"Yes, I'm sure." Cordelia snaps out the impatient response so quickly, the whole class goes silent at her audacity. "It's an urban myth. And a stupid one at that."

are signs asking the visitors not to tap on the glass, she does it anyhow. Then she spreads her fingers and presses her palm to the glass.

And the jellyfish come to her.

It doesn't happen quickly--and it could easily be coincidence--but somehow I doubt it. The creatures slowly gather at the center of the tank to surround her in a murky halo.

When she moves her hand along the glass, their bodies sway in that direction.

"I'm not studying jellyfish." Even to my ears, my voice sounds annoyed. So I soften it before she gives me that injured look again. "I want to study something else."

"Whatever you want, Kate." Her voice is distant. She doesn't care.

How unexpected.

But I'm not going to argue with her. Instead, I hug my notebook to my chest and walk away. A part of me thinks she'll call me back, and my ears strain for it, but for once, Cordelia leaves me alone.

When I turn the corner, a new set of tanks await me. I decide to pick one and be done with it.

In spite of everything, a small prickle of interest rears its head when I spot the electric eel. There's a gauge above the tank. Every time the eel touches the metal bars inside the tank, the voltage registers. Interesting, and easily

measurable for my report.

The electric eel it is.

I drop my bag on the bench in front of the tank. I pull out a pen and open my notebook to a blank page, record the start time, and copy the blurb on the sign, along with all the pertinent scientific information.

Five minutes passes, and the eel does nothing other than swim back and forth. I've got a column of voltage readings which don't vary all that much. The creature isn't nearly as interesting as I'd hoped, and Wuthering Heights is calling me.

"Mind if I join you?"

The voice is simultaneously familiar and impossible, because it belongs to Jason Crawford. I find the composure to shrug and turn back to the tank. To feign indifference because anything else would be mortifying.

"My grandfather used to go fishing all the time." Jason drops his bag on the ground and settles on the bench next to me. "He once caught an electric eel. He says it shocked the shit out of him when he tried to remove it from the hook."

"Did it hurt?" The question is inane, but nothing else comes to mind. And I have no idea why he's talking to me. Light flickers off his strong jaw, and although I can't see his eyes, I know they're a startling hazel with long eyelashes.

He nods. "So I've always been curious

about them. And this is as good a time as any to watch them, right?" He begins copying down all the same information that I have.

I need to say something. Or else he'll think I'm retarded or socially awkward or something.

"So why did you pick them?" he says.

I shrug. "Because I didn't want to do what everyone else is doing."

Now he's watching me, but I keep my eyes on the swimming eel.

"You're Kate, aren't you? I've seen you hanging around that strange girl. Clarissa or something, right?"

Strange girl? Heat flashes into my cheeks. Whether the embarrassment is for myself or for Cordelia, I have no idea. If he thinks she's strange, does that mean I'm strange by proxy? I could deny our friendship, but that might be worse, for surely everyone has seen us eating lunch together (if they noticed us at all.) And I'm not a liar.

"Her name is Cordelia."

But Jason waves the name away with a dismissive gesture. "Have you ever been to one of our swim meets?"

Yes. All of them. Religiously. But that isn't something I can say. "A few."

"Are you coming tonight?"

I bite my lip and doodle a mark on the edge of my paper. What should I say? "Maybe." ✴

I usually drag Cordelia to the swim meets just to have someone to sit with. Tonight, however, I decide to go without her, even though being alone goes against every high school rule there is.

This afternoon, when she found me next to Jason, she interrupted to chatter about her goddamn jellyfish. She ignored his presence completely.

Why was she judging me? How was it any better for her to be obsessed with jellyfish than it was for me to be obsessed with Jason?

The stands are crowded, but I've chosen a seat near the middle of the indoor stadium. A group of girls from my French class are next to me, so at least it won't look like I'm alone if Jason happens to see me.

Not that he'll be looking for me anyhow. The interlude at the aquarium was what my Prob & Stat teacher would call an outlier. An unforeseen and random event outside the normal parameters which could be ignored.

I'll probably never speak to him again, but that doesn't matter.

I want to be here.

To my surprise, however, Jason does see me. When the team comes through the gym doors and onto the concrete surrounding the pool, the group of them pause for applause. His gaze alights on my face, and he smiles.

Unwittingly, I smile back.

Which is, of course, when Cordelia collapses next to me.

"Whew!" Her face is flushed, and her hair is stuck to her temples with sweat. Was she running or something? "Boy this place is crowded!"

"What are you doing here?" The question pops out before I have time to think about it.

Her mouth drops open slightly. "We always come here, Kate. You didn't call, but I assumed we'd come tonight, so here I am."

I stay silent, and so does she. I feel guilty, and I'm not sure why. I don't know what to say to her, and it seems like she's feeling that same kind of uncertainty. But if she brings up the jellyfish, I'll lose it.

The team does well against our competitors. Jason even manages to score the fastest time during one of the events, which is enough to put our school in the lead at the end. I cheer just as loudly as everyone else, which causes my so-called friend to frown.

"Why do you like him?"

"Who says I like him?"

She sighs. "Kate. It's obvious."

My cheeks heat. Obvious to everyone? Is that what she means? Is that why Jason was nice to me? Because everyone already knows about my silly little crush?

Suddenly, I feel foolish. What's wrong with me? Of course Jason isn't interested

110

in me. He's a friendly guy who was just making conversation this afternoon, and I was seriously reading way too much into it. But I still can't explain those feelings to Cordelia, who's never had a crush on anything other than a floating blob.

"It's okay," Cordelia says. "I was going to go home and start my report, but maybe we can watch Pride and Prejudice instead. If you want to, I mean." The last sentence is tacked on, like she isn't sure how I'll react to her invitation.

Or if I'm going to throw it back in her face.

It's kind of her to offer an alternative, so I agree. The two of us slowly weave through the crowd. This isn't the way I'd imagined the evening would go, and I'm unbelievably, stupidly disappointed.

"Kate!"

I turn at the sound of my name. To my surprise, Jason is making his way through the crowd. His hair is wet and spiky, and he smells like chlorine, but he seems happy to see me.

Which instantly improves my mood.

Cordelia lets out an impatient sigh. She glances at her watch, gives me a pointed look and glares at the interloping boy in our midst.

"You're not leaving, are you?" he says.

"We were just about to." My smile

must be enormous, but it's all I can do to contain myself. It's one thing for him to interact with me in the dark, secluded aquarium away from his friends.

It's quite another for him to flag me down after a swim meet where he's the hero.

"We're having a party at Brandon's house tonight." Someone claps Jason on his shoulder, and he's momentarily distracted by another well-wisher. But when he turns back to me, he grasps my upper arm. "You should come."

I want to say yes. But Cordelia's expression catches my attention and I can't do it. As frustrating as she can be, I'm supposed to be her friend, and I can't abandon her like this.

Can I?

"Well…" and my voice trails off. How can I explain it without coming across as a complete bitch? I can't just invite Cordelia along, but I can't go without her either. Nor can I wave her off like she's second best and ride off into the sunset with my favorite swimmer.

But I want to go. More than anything. How many opportunities would I miss if I turned him down? He probably wouldn't ask me again. I had to say yes.

Didn't I?

In the end, Cordelia makes the decision for me. "It's fine, Kate. I need to go home and get started on my project. Have a nice time." Her voice is wooden, and she's already started walking away.

Is it wrong to feel both guilt and relief?

I wasted most of the weekend daydreaming about Jason. Although I spent very little time at the party--and only a few minutes talking to him--the scene keeps repeating in my head, over and over for the entire week.

Whenever I try to bring up the party, Cordelia changes the subject. Most often, she babbles about her jellyfish project, and then I'm the one who changes the subject.

A week after our assignments are turned in, the teacher announces that some of the students had done such a good job, she'd like those students to present their papers.

Cordelia is one of them.

She's even dressed up for her presentation. Her jean skirt is long and dark, and it doesn't fit her all that well. Cordelia has tiny feet, made even smaller by the penny loafers. The contrast between her feet and her thick mid-section makes her look even heavier than usual.

But she is excited, so I try to be happy for her. I give her a reassuring smile as she stands up and moves to the front of the class. Finally, she gets the chance to tell everyone about her favorite creatures. Maybe this will get rid of her obsession. Maybe she won't need to talk about them so incessantly.

At least I can hope.

She's assembled a Powerpoint presentation with tons of photos of jellyfish. All the different kinds, close-ups of stinging cells, drawings of life cycles. Her enthusiasm for the subject is simultaneously admirable and embarrassing, but everyone seems to be paying attention, and I'm glad for that. No matter what my current feelings towards her are, I don't want other people to make fun of her.

So it's inevitable, I suppose, that everything goes to shit when she asks if there are any questions.

Two desks away from me, Doug Bryson raises his hand. There's a smirk on his face which is as familiar to me as my own reflection. Doug plays pretty much every sport there is, and he's captain or highest scorer for nearly all of them, including the swim team. He always dates the hottest girls, and he's a serious asshole.

Unfortunately, he's also brilliant, which adds another level to his cruelty.

"So I have a question," he says.

A few of his fans snicker, and a sick feeling wells up within my stomach. Cordelia's face is blank. She doesn't seem nervous, but I'm feeling enough of it to make up for her.

"Is it true you're supposed to piss on a jellyfish sting?"

Giggles erupt. The teacher hushes

112

them, but not before Cordelia answers.

"No, that's not true. Urine doesn't work. You need to use something more acidic to keep the nematocysts from firing. Salt water or vinegar will do in a pinch."

"Are you sure? Because a surfer friend of mine swears that--"

"Yes, I'm sure." Cordelia snaps out the impatient response so quickly, the whole class goes silent at her audacity. "It's an urban myth. And a stupid one at that."

Dead silence.

I stare at Doug, whose face has frozen in an odd expression. I can't tell if he's pissed or amazed or shocked at this chubby, unpopular girl daring to suggest that he might have said something stupid.

I have to say, I'm almost proud of her.

By lunchtime, everyone is calling Cordelia the Jellyfish Queen.

She's gone from obscurity to notoriety in the span of three hours. Unbelievable.

I can't stop looking at her, even though she's the one with her head buried in a book instead of me. She's the one ignoring everyone. Aside from the slight flush to her cheeks, she doesn't appear much affected by all the shit Doug has thrown her way since this morning's presentation. All the comments about her hair, her clothing, the jellyfish and whether she'd stop firing her nematocysts if someone pisses on her.

She must have caught him off-guard. He's usually more witty.

"You did a good job on your presentation." I don't know what else to say when she's like this. Is she upset? Is she angry?

There was a time when I would have known. A few years ago. Maybe even a few months ago. Now I have no idea what she's thinking, but I want her to feel better. This attention has to bother her. It bothers me, and it's not even directed at me.

Cordelia looks up. Her eyes are narrowed. "Really?"

I nod. "Of course. Yours was the best. The most interesting."

"You're not just saying that, are you? Because you don't need to stay stuff like that if you don't mean it."

"No, I mean it." And I do.

Cordelia stares at me as though she's trying to sense my sincerity. In the end, she must believe me, because she smiles and lets out a sigh. "Can you believe everything that's happened?"

"Doug's an asshole. It'll pass."

She nods her agreement, and for the remainder of the lunch hour, it's like the jellyfish don't exist anymore. And we're still the best of friends.

Except it doesn't pass. Doug doesn't let it drop.

In fact, he keeps getting worse. Every day, he harasses Cordelia before school, between classes and after school. The name-calling reaches new levels of immaturity. Jellyfish graffiti appears on her locker, on her desks and on one occasion, on her homework assignment. To be honest, I'm having trouble understanding why he's so angry with her. Why he's so focused on a girl who should have been beneath his notice. Why he's devoting so much energy to someone who barely insulted him.

Cordelia tries to ignore it. She's more dignified about it than I would have thought possible. If I'd been the brunt of Doug's rage, I probably would have taken the week off school in the hopes he'd lose interest. Having lunch with Cordelia has gotten more difficult too. I can feel the eyes of the other students on us.

Do they pity the Jellyfish Queen? Or do they pity me for being her friend?

"I'm thinking about volunteering at the aquarium." Cordelia picks up a french fry, dips it in ketchup and pops it into her mouth.

I stare at her. "Are you crazy? That'll just make everything worse."

She gives me this look which I can't

describe. Then she leans in closer. "I'm not changing my life to suit Doug Bryson. If I want to volunteer at the aquarium, then I'll do it. And I don't need your permission or approval either, Kate."

Her words sting. "Fine. Do whatever you want." I wave my hand in the air to show how little I care.

I want to get up and walk away. I need to get away from her so badly it's a physical ache. Why is she still so obsessed with them? When the damn creatures have caused her so much angst, why is she still so blind?

I don't understand her. Perhaps I never did.

I haven't spoken to Jason since the weekend of the party. Somehow, that's even worse than the constant reminders of jellyfish all over the school. Of course, it's possible his silent treatment has everything to do with the jellyfish and nothing to do with me. Why would he want to be associated with me or Cordelia when Doug's vendetta is still in overdrive? I want to talk about the Jason situation, to hash things through, but Cordelia isn't receptive to boy talk, so I don't bother to bring it up.

"Are we going to the swim meet today?" Cordelia is smiling, like she knows something I don't. It's her way of

114

teasing me about Jason.

And I don't like it.

"No."

She blinks twice, and the smile dies from her face. "Why not?"

"Because I don't want to go."

"Because of Doug?"

Does she think I'm doing this for her? I'm not that generous. But I don't say that. She can think whatever she wants. She can assume it's all about her. "Let's do something else."

"We could watch Pride & Prejudice."

I shake my head before she's even finished saying the title. "I don't want to stay at home. Let's go somewhere. Do something different." Maybe going out would make me feel like less of a loser. I could pretend it was my choice not to see Jason.

Not his.

"Well..." Her gaze flickers up, and she seems uncertain. "We could go to the beach."

My immediate impulse is to say no. But then I hesitate. I used to like the beach. I look across the cafeteria, to the expanse of windows along the side. It's actually sunny outside instead of perpetually gloomy.

"Okay."

Cordelia and I cut the last two classes of the day. I'm surprised she's agreed, but perhaps it has something to do with Doug Bryson in her last period English class.

We stop off at our houses to change into our bathing suits. Neither of my parents are home, so no uncomfortable explanations are necessary there, and Cordelia's mom is too busy painting in her studio to notice her daughter's home early.

When we get to the beach, Cordelia sets her bag and towel down about twenty feet from a cove. Corpses of jellyfish are strewn along the sand. The sight of them makes me groan.

I can't get away from them.

My bag gets dropped next to Cordelia's, and then I roll out my towel. The sun feels good against my skin, so I quickly remove my shirt and shorts, slap on a little lotion, lay down and close my eyes.

Beside me, I can hear Cordelia mimicking my movements, although she remains sitting upright. I can tell by the light flickering across my eyelids.

"I'm starting my internship at the aquarium tomorrow."

Of course she is.

But I don't say anything. All I do is let out a grunt of acknowledgment because the last time we talked about this, she snapped at me.

"I'm working with this woman. She's a doctor of invertebrate anatomy, although she specializes in aquatic creatures. Isn't that cool?"

Not really.

Again with the grunt.

I can hear Cordelia brushing sand off her skin. I open my eyes to see her frowning down at me.

"What's going on with you, Kate? We used to spend every afternoon together. We used to talk on the phone every night. Now, you barely even look at me, and getting you to talk is like pulling teeth."

I can't repress a sigh as I sit up. "You're wrong, Cordelia. We do talk. It's just always about the freaking jellyfish. I don't know what's left to say about them, and frankly, they bore the shit out of me."

Her face flushes. "Well, what should we talk about then? Your little crush on Jason Crawford? Everyone knows he's with Celeste Harding. There's nothing going on between you and him."

"You think I don't know that? Why do you think I came here with you instead of going to the swim meet?"

She goes silent, and there's an injured puppy dog look to her eyes.

Cordelia always brings out the worst in me.

"I'm going for a swim." She stands up and strides down to the water. Her bathing suit is yellow and not very flattering against her fish-white skin. Her limp hair barely rises even though the wind has started to pick up.

I can't watch her anymore. Instead, I

115

lie back down on my towel, cover my eyes with my forearm and imagine a world without jellyfish.

"You didn't come to the swim meet."

I jerk upright, disturbed to have fallen asleep at the beach. Cordelia's stuff is still next to me, although she's absent.

The voice belongs to Jason Crawford.

"What time is it?" I ask him.

"About six."

Shit. How could I have fallen asleep for three hours? And where was Cordelia?

He sits down on the sand next to my towel. His hair is rumpled and damp, although the fact that he's fully dressed makes me self-conscious. I feign a chill and drag my shirt over my head. Jason watches me with an expression that makes me blush.

I'm not as pretty as Celeste.

"You didn't come to the swim meet."

"Was I supposed to?"

He shrugs and strokes the sand. Lifts up a handful and allows it to sift to the ground, smoothes out the surface and does it all over again. It's mesmerizing. "I just thought you'd be there."

I want to ask him why he cares, but I can't. "Did the team win?"

"Yeah."

I look away from him, and my gaze

116

snags on Cordelia. She's waist-deep in the water, although it looks like she's making her way back to the beach. Has she been swimming all this time?

"We're having a bonfire tonight to celebrate." He motions towards the other side of the beach, where a group of people are gathered around a large pile of wood. Two guys in multi-colored shorts are trying to light it. Large coolers are strewn around the area, along with a few kegs. Suddenly I regret my decision to come to the beach.

I stand up and wave to Cordelia, hoping she doesn't ignore me. She nods her agreement and begins to surge towards shore. I have no desire to be here while the swim team celebrates a victory. In this, Cordelia and I are united.

"You should come." Jason stands up and brushes sand off his shorts.

"I don't think so." I pick up my towel and sand goes flying everywhere. I shake it out as best I can before rolling it up and tucking it inside my bag.

"Why not?"

The reason is obvious to anyone other than Jason, apparently.

"Because."

His gaze narrows. "Why not, Kate?"

When Cordelia returns, she barely looks at him and silently gathers her things together. That's when I notice the plastic bags filled with some weird whitish substance.

And that's all I can see. Jason doesn't exist anymore. Neither does Cordelia herself. Just the goddamn jellyfish my fucked-up friend gathered into ordinary sandwich bags.

She planned this. This trip to the beach had nothing to do with me.

Rage fills my blood so fierce I can't even speak.

"Is something wrong?" Jason says.

I want to scream at her, but instead I turn towards him. "I'll meet you down at the bonfire, okay? Just give me a minute." When he gets out of earshot, I turn back to my so-called friend.

Cordelia has her bag clamped over her chest, and she looks both defensive and annoyed. "I guess you've made your decision then."

"No, you made it for me." I point at the bag.

She looks down at her backpack, and then back up at me. "Fine." Her face has gone white, and her voice is raspy. "You want to be friends with the people who've been so awful to me? I don't give a shit anymore."

Then she leaves. And I feel like the biggest bitch in the world.

The weekend passes in a blur. Cordelia doesn't return my calls, I have no idea what will happen today at school, and a part of me doesn't care because Jason drove me home following the beach incident.

On Saturday night, we spent the evening chatting on the phone and instant messaging.

On Sunday afternoon, we saw a movie and he kissed me afterwards. My first real kiss. Is it wrong to be so happy at a time like this?

But today is Monday, and things will be different. Cordelia's car is in the parking lot, so I know she's not skipping school, but she doesn't show up for biology or for lunch. No one comments on her absence--not even Doug Bryson-- and it's like the Jellyfish Queen no longer exists.

In any case, I'm looking forward to this afternoon. Jason has invited me to watch the team practice. What else am I going to do after school? Call Cordelia for the twelfth time and let her ignore me again?

I don't think so.

The stadiums are less packed than they'd been during the match. Even so, groups of people are scattered along the bleachers and down around the pool area. I pick a seat near the middle to watch the swimmers.

There's something so graceful about their movements. So fluid and repetitious, it's like being lulled into a trance. My gaze is most often drawn to Jason, of course. But Doug Bryson catches my attention too, and not just because of the Cordelia situation. When

117

he's swimming against his teammates, it's obvious why he's the best.

His strokes are stronger, quicker and more elegant. He's so talented and it's so unfair.

Only fate can explain why I look away from the pool in the split second when Cordelia appears at the gym entrance. Surprise leaks into my veins. What's she doing here?

I almost call out to her, but something holds me back. Whether that something is about not drawing attention to myself or to her is uncertain. Regardless, I stay silent and watch her walk to the edge of the pool.

Two of the lanes are roped off for general swimming, reserved for the students just looking for exercise without a coach to scream at them. Right now, those lanes are empty save a cluster of chattering girls in the shallow end and a freshman practicing the breaststroke.

No one sees Cordelia crouch at the edge of the pool. She's holding something in her hand, but she submerges it before I can identify what it is. When her hand comes back up, there's nothing there.

She wasn't just testing the water. I know it.

Cordelia stands. Her lips move, but I can't hear the words.

Then she looks up, directly at me. As though she was destined to do so. A slow

118

smile curls over her lips as she raises her dripping hand in the air for a wave.

Abruptly, she turns, walks back to the door and exits the gym.

The screams begin a minute later.

Half of the swim team has been stung, but Doug Bryson is by far the worst. The jellyfish seem to have taken a perverse liking to him. His face is angry red, blistered and swollen; he's barely recognizable when he's taken to the hospital.

Everyone is asking how the jellyfish could have made it into the pool.

Fear tightens my body into inaction. Long after the place has emptied of everyone except the people from animal control, I'm still up in the stands.

No one seems to have seen her. One of the swimmers mentions the Jellyfish Queen, but no one verifies her presence at the scene. No one saw her enter. No one saw her leave. And one person claims that she wasn't even in school today. The school officials promise to find out how this happened, but they know Cordelia and her impressive academic record and already they're certain she wasn't responsible.

I know differently. But I say nothing.

Jason calls me that evening. He's one of the few swimmers the jellyfish didn't touch. He went to the hospital with the others, having forgotten all about me.

Another girl might have been angry about that. Not me. Not when Cordelia had just used her jellyfish army (or would it be navy?) to attack the swim team. I'm not in any kind of mood to talk about what happened, so I just listen to him rant about the pain suffered by his fellow swimmers.

Then he brings it up. Because he has to. I expect the subject, but I still cringe when her name finally crosses his lips.

"That girl, Cordelia." He waits for me to say something, but I remain silent. "People are saying she did this."

"I know."

He sighs. Is he exasperated with me? "Did she?"

"How would I know?"

"Isn't she your friend?"

My grip tightens on the phone. "Well, yeah. But I haven't spoken to her since Friday. Besides, no one saw her at the pool."

Skirting the truth twists my stomach with guilt. Ten years of friendship with Cordelia versus a weekend's relationship with Jason, and yet I'm still tempted to tell him.

He drops the subject in favor of discussing the injuries some more. I don't want to hear the details, but I listen anyhow. Penance, I suppose, for not speaking up against Cordelia. When Jason hangs up, I feel like he's annoyed with me. Perhaps he senses that I'm protecting my friend.

Almost as soon as we hang up, the phone rings again.

Cordelia.

I could ignore her. I could send the Jellyfish Queen straight to voicemail.

But curiosity and anger win out.

"Cordelia."

"Kate."

Why does she sound angry with me? None of this is my fault. When did she get so self-righteous? So Doug Bryson humiliated her. So what?

Did that really justify her actions?

"I know what you did."

"Do you?" I can hear the smile in her voice. "Good luck proving it."

"They already know it's you. Everyone's been talking about the Jellyfish Queen since it happened."

"Don't you dare call me that. You, of all people, don't need to call me that."

For the first time, I start to wonder if she hates me just as much as I've grown to hate her.

"Why did you do it?"

She lets out an impatient noise. "Don't play stupid, Kate. And keep your mouth shut unless you want to become the next outcast. No one saw anything. No one will accuse me of anything."

Her tone is really starting to piss me off.

"And if I don't?"

119

"Think about it, Kate. Your boyfriend got off scot-free. Do you think that was an accident?"

I can't think of a single thing to say. Is that a threat? Or am I supposed to be grateful somehow?

Cordelia sighs. "You never used to be so obtuse. Meet me at the beach after school tomorrow, and I'll explain." Then she hangs up.

School is weird the next day. A few of the swimmers are back in class, showing off their war wounds. There are rumors floating about Cordelia, but she isn't there to hear them. No one has come forward to say that she did it, and the tide of gossip seems to favor a rival swim team as responsible.

The thing is, if Cordelia had simply kept her mouth shut, I wouldn't have any trouble keeping mine shut either. The length of our friendship demands loyalty, and I wouldn't have thrown her to the sharks.

I'm still going to give her a chance to explain. One chance to make things right.

And then I'll walk away from the Jellyfish Queen forever.

At the beach, Cordelia turns and looks down at me. Her hand rises in a half-hearted wave, and her smile flickers, like she's nervous. Or perhaps it's hard for her to smile at me with any

sincerity.

"What do you want, Cordelia?"

The smile is gone now. "I'm trying to remember, Kate. Were you always this bitchy? Or has it been a more recent transformation?"

So she's on the attack then? I can fight back too.

"I don't know. Perhaps it started right around the time you turned psycho about jellyfish."

She's shaking her head. "You still don't get it, do you? I almost feel sorry for you."

"Get what?" Frustration overwhelms me. "What is there to get? The fact that you're incapable of talking about anything that doesn't have 'tentacles?'" Here I make quote marks with my fingers.

She inhales a sharp breath.

"Or the fact that you almost killed Doug Bryson?"

The accusation hangs in the air like a cloud. And she doesn't look sorry at all. Her jaw is set at that stubborn angle, and her eyes flash with irritation.

"None of that matters." She brushes it all away with a wave of her hand. "That isn't why I wanted to meet you here."

"Then why?"

"To say goodbye."

A weird feeling clenches my chest. Relief? Dismay? I can't tell.

"Where are you going?"

120

She smiles. "An internship with the aquarium. That scientist I told you about? She wants me to be her assistant when she goes to Hawaii for research."

It's everything Cordelia has ever wanted. A million questions spring to mind. Questions that any concerned friend should ask. What about finishing high school? Where will she stay? What do her parents think? Will she be okay?

I should say something. Her expression has gotten uncomfortable the longer I stay silent. "I'm happy for you."

She acknowledges the wooden sentiment with a nod. "We'll keep in touch, right?"

"Sure."

There doesn't seem to be anything left to say. There's no point in discussing what happened at the pool. And we won't keep in touch. I know that as surely as I know my own name. And I can't stop it any more than I can stop the tide from surging on the shore.

"Good luck with your jellyfish." I lean forward and give her a quick hug because it seems like the thing to do.

"Good luck with Jason."

Cordelia's mother calls two days later. Do I know where Cordelia has gone?

I tell her about the aquarium. Her mother knows nothing about it, and subsequent calls to the aquarium yield nothing. Cordelia hasn't volunteered there, let alone been asked to go on a research trip to Hawaii.

She lied about everything.

Today, I'm back at the beach. The jellyfish corpses have disappeared from the sand, although that doesn't really matter. I'm looking for something else.

Eventually, I find a backpack shoved in-between two rocks. I pull it out and search its contents. A familiar green jacket. Empty specimen bags. A yellow bathing suit, a towel and all the clothing Cordelia wore that day.

I know what other people will say. She drowned. Or she ran away.

They're wrong, of course. But better for them to speculate. Better for me to keep my mouth shut about this as well.

At least that's what I tell myself as I toss her clothing into the ocean.

Perhaps the Jellyfish Queen will find it some day.

The City at Night

by
Jeremy Schliewe

Herein... mystery and beauty... a glimpse of

After Ben's eyes had adjusted to the darkness they found themselves repeatedly pulled to the corner of the room, where a diffuse, distracting light cast a warm glow that climbed the lower reaches of the meeting walls. He batted his eyelids, as if the light were some malfunction in the effort of rods and cones or an annoyance that could be blinked away, but behind the gentle slope of his blanketed right foot it remained. It was as if, as perhaps a sort of practical joke, someone had stolen into his bedroom and plugged a night-light into the socket, bathing the corner of the darkened room in a dull orange light. But what would be the motivation behind such a stunt? The implied invasion of space and privacy could have darker underpinnings to be sure, but Benjamin Clark, who in life bore in silence the barbs and blades of coworkers, friends, and family, was not the type of man to have enemies.

He thought of Janeane. Was it

possible she had planted the night-light as a gesture of affection? It was all but impossible, a night thought he wouldn't even entertain in the daylight hours. She had never been to his place. He doubted that she knew his neighborhood. It was better not to let his thoughts wander in that particular direction. It was difficult to imagine such a woman, with her tight curls and eyeglasses, her gangly frame softened by professional skirts and jackets, engaged in the act of breaking and entering, no matter how noble or romantic the reason behind it may be. Ben pulled the blanket and sheet off his supine body, got out of bed, and took three steps to the corner of the room to investigate the emanation.

He was puzzled to find a small building, no more than nine inches tall, sitting atop the carpeting. Its lights were on--this was the source of the glow. The building was exceedingly modern, a skyscraper in miniature, facaded entirely in tinted glass in which Ben, on hands and knees, could see the features of his lean face darkly reflected. Peering through the windows, he saw floors with glossy tiles, rows and rows of desks and chairs mazed by cubicle walls, all under the glow of florescent lights that, housed in plastic, tracked the ceiling from back to front. As far as Ben could see, no one was inside, not a night watchman nor a lonely janitor pushing a cart, not a worker staying on past quitting time. It was the middle of the night, after all.

More striking was that the building, though fixed in space, was translucent-- only seventy-five percent or so there. If he held his open palm behind the building, he could see its faint form through the skyscraper. If the skyscraper were only partially there to the eye, it was even less so to the touch. When Ben put a tentative finger to the building to test its surface, he was not entirely surprised when it passed through the windows, floors, ceilings, and everything else as if they were made of air. The building had all the properties of a hologram, though Ben's humble bedroom contained no device capable of projecting such a thing.

He spent the better part of an hour with the building before he grew sleepy. It stood in the corner, mutely asserting its territory, as if it had every right to be there and no plans to leave anytime soon. Ben crawled back into bed and closed his eyes to the orange aura in the corner. It was puzzling, to be sure, but it seemed to be harmless. He returned to bed and fell asleep. When he awoke the next morning the sun was up and the skyscraper gone.

The memory of the building lingered throughout Ben's morning ritual but faded shortly after he set out for work. Janeane sat slouched behind the large, semicircular counter at the end of a gray expanse of commercial carpeting, worrying a pen cap between her teeth. She sat upright, clapped the pen onto the countertop, and smiled as Ben entered the building. As he approached, he could see her squint in his direction through her eyeglasses, the lenses of which were already considerably thick.

"You look tired," she said.

"I had some trouble getting to sleep."

Between them hung a silence not unlike that of last Thursday night, when, before the concrete steps of Janeane's home, Ben planted an awkward kiss on the corner of her

After Janeane's second glass of champagne, she tucked her feet under Ben's thighs to warm them. He felt her wiggle her toes. She wants a kiss, he thought. He drained the rest of his glass for courage and when he turned toward her he saw her eyes were closed and she had fallen asleep.

125

mouth, said that he'd call soon, and set out in the wrong direction in search of his car.

In his office, Ben stacked and re-stacked the papers on his desk. He cleaned out each drawer and put all the loose paperclips back in their small container. At ten thirty-three, he picked up his phone and called the front desk.

"Janeane? This is Ben. I was wondering if you would like to see a movie Friday night?"

He wrote the date in on Friday's space on his desk calendar and didn't get much done for the rest of the day. At home Ben microwaved a frozen lasagna dinner, ate two ice cream sandwiches, flipped through the television channels, and surfed the internet before weariness prompted him to shuffle to the bathroom and brush his teeth a half an hour earlier than was his habit.

With the lights out and Ben under the blankets, the skyscraper that had appeared in the corner of the room the night before returned. Though Ben had not carried the memory of the apparition throughout the motions of the day, the light in the corner of the room immediately struck him as brighter than it had been the night before. Getting out of bed, he saw the reason for the increased brightness-- three new buildings had joined the skyscraper. The most striking addition was even taller than the original reflective building. It looked older, like something that had been erected in the early part of the twentieth century, and was topped with an art deco spire.

Inspecting the carpet, Ben saw the perimeter of each building was hugged by sidewalks and streets. An intersection was spanned by a wire upon which was hung a traffic light that winked green, yellow, red. The quartet glowed warmly in the gloom. A city was forming at the foot of his bed.

Each night Ben found the number of buildings had grown. From the bottom right corner of his bed, the city grew to the left and by Thursday night nearly covered its width. In anticipation he found himself going to bed earlier, when the darkness outside had deepened to the point of saturation, for the city never appeared earlier. In his pajamas he would lie on his stomach and watch over the foot of the bed, resting his chin on crossed arms until sleep overtook him. Through their translucence he could see where the carpeting met the sliding doors of the closet. Should he awaken in the middle of the night with a full bladder, he would be in no danger of kicking over the buildings or trampling them underfoot. The city was no more concrete than it had been since the first building appeared.

At work it became increasingly difficult to push the thought of the growing city from his mind. He looked forward to seeing the new developments that waited for him in the absence of light. He anticipated looking down on the development from over the horizon of his mattress. There was something in this exchange that made Ben feel like a god, though if he were playing some part in the creation of the city it was certainly not on any conscious level. There came with it a feeling of peace, such as Ben had never experienced. It was as if he were a projection of something larger that was happening beyond his perception--and the love he felt for what he was witnessing seemed an indication of a greater benevolence.

After the movie, Janeane wanted to see Ben's apartment. The thought that he would be having company that night hadn't struck him, so Ben scoured the refrigerator and the pantry in hopes of finding something to drink, but it was rare that he kept alcohol. He put a pot of water on the burner to heat for tea.

"We should have stopped at the store," Janeane said. She looked disappointed.

"There's a gas station on the corner," Ben said. He opened the refrigerator in the hope that something had materialized since his last inspection. The crisper: he hadn't thought to look there. He didn't stock enough food to merit its everyday use but sometimes found it useful for long-term storage. He pulled it open and examined the contents--two plastic canisters with film for a camera he no longer owned, an unopened eight-pack of double-A batteries, and a leftover bottle of champagne, forced on him after his brother's wedding reception the previous August.

Janeane smiled when he held up the bottle. He took the pot of water from the burner, poured the champagne into two mismatched tumblers, and took a seat next to Janeane on the couch. She had taken off her glasses and set them upturned on the end table, an effect that made her eyes seem small and squinty. After one glass of the champagne she had kicked off her shoes and sat with her legs neatly folded, absently petting one of her bare feet. Ben looked at the wall opposite the couch and wondered what was happening in his bedroom on the other side. Was it possible that his presence was required for the city's continued growth?

"You're not very talkative," Janeane observed.

"Oh?" Ben said. "I guess I've had a lot on my mind lately."

"It's work," she said. "I remind you of work. I was afraid this would be a problem."

Ben laughed. "It's not that at all."

127

After Janeane's second glass of champagne, she tucked her feet under Ben's thighs to warm them. He felt her wiggle her toes. She wants a kiss, he thought. He drained the rest of his glass for courage and when he turned toward her he saw her eyes were closed and she had fallen asleep. Not wanting to wake her, he got a blanket and extra pillow from the hall closet. He covered her and kissed her on the forehead. Janeane stirred and quietly murmured an apology.

"It's okay," Ben said. "I'll take you home whenever you want."

She moved herself so that she lay on her side against the back cushions and patted the space on the couch she had created. "I want you to lie down."

Ben did and Janeane kissed him warmly on the mouth. "Next time," she said, "we'll have to start that sooner."

She soon fell asleep again and Ben could not resist the temptation to steal into his room and check the progress of his miniature city. He climbed on to the bed to reclaim his familiar vantage and was startled to see that, though the city nearly spanned the width of his bed as it had the night before, no new skyscrapers had appeared in the leftward progression. There were forty-seven, exactly the number of the night before. Ben's heart sank. Had his lack of attention somehow stopped the city's growth? Was it some sort of punishment

128

for having Janeane over?

Then he saw it. Looking down it was difficult to discern the new features from his dark carpeting. He had been looking for skyscrapers, after all, so the rectangular lawns and black shingled roofs of the suburbs were easily lost next to the teeming city. Ben rolled out of bed and got on the floor for a closer look.

The suburb, as if to dissuade the eye from seeing the grid of a planned community, was intersticed with streets that lazily arced back and forth--so that if one did see a lattice it was as if through looking through a warping layer of water. A handful of cul-de-sacs were thrown in as if to break the monotonous pattern, but when viewed from above the repetition was as obvious as the modified crisscrossing streets. The houses, gray and trimmed with white, each with an electric lamp shining sentry by the brick path to the front door, were set on hills. Driveways were made of two ample slabs of concrete at obtuse angles, as if hinged to accommodate the ascent and leveling to the spacious garages. Apparently, as in life, the city wasn't for everyone.

Ben spent the rest of the weekend alone. The suburb completed itself over the next two nights.

Would anybody else, if invited into his room at night, be able to see the city? Ben was not sure, but he had a feeling it wouldn't be long until Janeane would want to see his bedroom. His place was the logical choice--on their dates she often complained of a roommate that spent hours upon hours in the living room with two cats and a blaring television.

Bypassing the suburbs, a winding, two-lane road with a bright double line down the middle snaked its way out of the city. Scrub vegetation lined the road on either side and at intervals long driveways shot away and led to squat houses. Ben counted four of them.

At the office, Ben's distraction increased. The nights he had been spending poised on the bed, surveying the still city on the floor, had kept him from getting the proper amount of sleep. Often, after lunch, he would not be able to focus on work at all. In a half-dreamlike state he would fall into a habit of peering over the edge of the desk and populating the room with buildings, streets, and houses. If a city were to appear here in the office, he asked himself, what would it look like? He was not able to come up with anything as fixed as was his city in the bedroom. What he could create in the office was shifting, ethereal, clearly the work of a preoccupied imagination--that which awaited him in the nighttime was

something else entirely; the buildings, once established, though invisible in daylight, never moved from the places they had first appeared, so that the arrangement was the same every night. The only change that occurred was in the right-to-left growth of the city, as if it had always existed but under a sheet that obscured it from view. Now, night after night, that sheet was being slowly pulled from the illusion it housed.

On the day he telephoned Janeane for a date--she had to decline on the grounds that she was flying home to visit her parents over the weekend--Ben was visited by a man from Human Resources.

"We understand you've been having trouble," the HR man said.

"What kind of trouble?" Ben asked. He was uncertain whether the man was referring to his dip in output or his nascent relationship with Janeane--it was against company policy for employees to date. If anyone found out, either Janeane or Ben could face a transfer to another city or, if transfer proved to be inconvenient for the company, termination.

"We don't like to lose employees," the HR man said, ignoring his question. "Especially when an early intervention can clear up a matter before it becomes a problem."

Ben leaned forward in his chair to let the HR man know he was listening. The

129

HR man pulled a pack of stick-it notes from the desktop toward him, produced a pen from his breast pocket, and wrote down a telephone number. He pushed the pad across the desktop so Ben could see it.

"We think you should call this number," he said.

Ben looked at the stick-it note as if he did not understand.

"It's someone for you to talk to," the HR man said.

The snaking road made a slow rise to the foothills of a mountain studded with evergreens. Pushed into the low mountain as if it were made of clay were a handful of elegant houses of varying modern design. Most were low-slung, with porches and rows of reflective windows that looked out on the countryside. One in particular that caught his eye was coral in color and perched over a steep upgrade. If I were to live anywhere on this landscape, Ben thought, that would be the place. He imagined the view he would have looking out from the porch, the pastel sunsets that gave way to darkness and the sparkling lights of the city below.

He slept through his alarm and woke up late for work. Forgoing breakfast and a shower, Ben still arrived twenty minutes late. His appointment with Doctor Godfrey, the company

130

psychologist, was in the afternoon. He spent the morning with his head on the desk, asleep.

Doctor Godfrey was in her mid-forties and wore a black sweater with a gray skirt and black stockings. She had a large nose and salt-and-pepper hair. Her smile was warm and eased some of the apprehension Ben had felt about seeing a therapist.

The first half hour of his session, he filled out a series of questionnaires in which he was asked to label a series of statements as true or false. Some were obviously designed to determine whether he was in the throes of depression (I no longer enjoy the activities I once enjoyed) or psychosis (My photograph is on the cover of several major publications). Once finished, Doctor Godfrey gave them a perfunctory glance and set them aside.

"What brings you here, Ben?"

"HR thought it was a good idea. My performance at work is suffering."

"Does this concern you?"

"Sure it does. I guess."

"Is there something that's changed in your personal life that might be having an effect on you?"

Ben thought it over and decided not to mention the city.

The next morning Ben called the front desk and told Janeane that he was taking a vacation day and would not be coming in to work. She seemed somewhat taken aback, though Ben quickly explained that it was simply a personal day to catch up on sleep. He spent most of the day at home, doing not much of anything other than a load of dishes and some light cleaning. For lunch he had a sandwich at a nearby coffee shop. Around sunset he took a short walk around his neighborhood.

He felt his city was in jeopardy, that it was such a delicate illusion that anything thrown out of balance in his life could change it or, worst of all, make it disappear altogether. He did not know what it meant or why it appeared, but that did not matter to him nearly as much as the fact that it was there for him at night. Perhaps if he could just spend enough time with it, any answer it could give would reveal itself. He fell naturally into the role of guardian. There was no doubt it had left him tired and was a distraction--his performance at work had suffered. There was only so much time in the day that one could be awake and full of energy. The visit from the HR man was the first step along on a path that ended with his termination. Why else would the company send him? Sure, it meant that they were taking steps to keep him--why else would they send him to Doctor Godfrey?--but if things didn't change the outcome would be obvious.

They were trying to entice him back. Turnover costs money and if a quick intervention could win Ben back, the company would be better off for it. But he was not ready to be won back. He needed time to think. He rarely took days off, so his vacation time was the perfect card to play. With it he could make work-time stop. Until his vacation it ran out, anyway.

He took the rest of the week off. Every night before bed he told himself that the next day he would rise with the alarm, perform his morning ritual, and go back to work. But each time he found himself calling Janeane and explaining that he would not be in. There was an increasing uneasiness in her voice. Perhaps, Ben thought, she was feeling that in abandoning work he was also abandoning her. It was not his intention, though at such an early stage in their relationship he did not feel comfortable sharing his intentions, be they noble or otherwise.

That week the city rewarded him with the most dazzling display. Night after night the mountain had slowly revealed itself, bending as it did around the foot of his bed and sloping upward as it neared his pillow. Here and there the mountain was stubbled with sparse forests of evergreen trees. Boulders studded the slopes. The crowning beauty was a wiry ski lift that ran along a stretch of pure white snow and ended near a quaint log cabin ski lodge, the windows of which threw rectangles of flickering firelight on the snow. A series of bluely shining lights were set in the frame of the ski lift. It was these hazy blue globes that illuminated the steady falling of snowflakes. Ben could watch this particular stretch of his bedroom landscape for hours, the falling of the silt-fine snow, the cable-hung empty chairs making their steady journey up and down the lift, the quiet wood of the cabin that hugged a blazing fire against the cold.

The back slope of the mountain was rockier, stubbled with thick pine forests, and faded as it descended toward the bedroom wall--the room allotted for no more growth in that direction. Ben took in the sight from right to left as it had revealed itself, the city, suburbs, scrub country, foothills, and snowy mountain, now visible as a whole. From the subtle shifts in traffic signals and window lights near the skyscrapers, to the cozy winter scene at his left, the apparition went about its quiet business. Ben felt blessed, as if he had somehow been chosen. The city was a gift. He understood it well enough to know just that, nothing more. It was a creation for which he could neither claim full responsibility nor deny playing any part in. His room, his mental state, and certainly factors of which he was not aware, had struck a balance and formed

132

something like a machine, something capable of populating his room with the scene that stretched out before him. His role fell somewhere in the middle, like that of an interpreter, akin to a laser reading information on a disc, the series ones and zeroes that could be translated into music or moving pictures.

Saturday evening Janeane showed up unannounced with a shopping bag full of cartons of Chinese takeout. She had been out running errands, she explained, and found herself in Ben's neighborhood and thought he might want something to eat. She had caught him off-guard. He had neither shaved nor showered that day and had spent the bulk of the day in a lazy circuit between his couch, on which he read a paperback novel, and his desk, searching an online archive of curious case studies in psychology in the hope that he would find something akin to his experience. He hadn't.

As Janeane arranged the food on the table, Ben put on a clean shirt, combed his hair, and washed his face. Feeling somewhat refreshed, he joined Janeane at the table.

"I'm sorry to barge in like this," she said.

"It's okay. I was getting hungry anyway." He twirled lo mein on his fork like he had with spaghetti noodles when he was a kid.

"People at work are talking," she said.

"Mm?"

"You're supposed to give the company more notice for your vacation time. You shouldn't be calling every day like that. Plus, who takes a vacation and doesn't go anywhere? It's weird."

"Then I'm weird," he said. "I'm a weird guy."

"I didn't mean it like that."

"It doesn't matter how you meant it. I'm admitting it right here and now." There was a shade of exasperation in his voice.

"I didn't mean to offend you," she said. "I shouldn't have come."

"It's not that," he said. "It has nothing to do with you. You'll just have to believe me."

"I should go." She pushed herself away from the table and stood up.

"Don't." Ben put his hand on her wrist. "I want you to stay," he said. "I'm just frustrated. It has nothing to do with you. I'm glad you're here."

It had come to the crucial point in which Ben was going to have to let her into his room or face the possibility that their relationship would die. Janeane's very presence made the decision less of a dilemma. When he was alone he could look at things more objectively--would she be able to see that which had formed in his room? Would she shatter the illusion and make it go away forever? She was a woman, willing and warm. She had taken a chance by showing up unannounced. She had exposed her feelings and her desire, and to send her away would require a level of coolness that Ben was incapable of gathering at the moment. He did, in his heart of hearts, desire Janeane and harbor feelings for her that did not stop at the physical. When he invited her into his bedroom he did so without any doubt that it was what he wanted.

He breathed a soft sigh as they crossed the threshold of the bedroom. The city and mountain were there, glowing faintly translucent in a soft bend around his bed. There was new growth. A river, lined by a rocky shore and foaming here and there in rapids, wended its way out from the foothills and toward the door. The illusion was so convincing that Ben found himself stepping over it in order to avoid getting his feet wet. So engrossed was he that he had failed to notice Janeane examining knickknacks on his chest of drawers, tiptoeing over to a small bookshelf and tenderly, as if it were made of spun glass, picking up a small framed photo of Ben's parents on their wedding day. It was clear that she saw nothing out of the ordinary.

They made love, quickly but tenderly, as if it were some business they had to get out of the way before moving on to other things. Ben sat partially up, propping himself on a folded pillow, while Janeane put a warm arm over his stomach and nuzzled his side. The scene was partially obscured by the bed, so Ben contented himself in observing the mountain. She could not see it after all. It certainly didn't feel like he had gone mad. There was too much a sense of peace that came with his nighttime apparition. He watched the snow falling as fine as mist, the silent chairs moving up and down the lift. Perhaps she would see it eventually. He would like to share it if he could, if only with one other person. Who better than Janeane, who spent her days behind that large semicircular desk fielding phone calls and greeting strangers, and, more often than not, went home to a microwaved dinner and a night of television. Maybe the city would be just what she needed. Given a little more time, maybe she would see it too.

At that moment, from a cluster of black-trunked pines, a family of miniature deer took tentative steps onto the fresh mountain snow. There was a buck, a doe, and two fawns with white spots like dabs of house paint standing out from their russet coats. The buck sported a fine rack of antlers and Ben could see clouds of steam that burst from its black nose as it exhaled fiercely into the cold.

134

When Ben's vacation time ran out, he began using his sick days. He and Janeane continued to see each other, and whenever she stayed with him he hoped she would see the city in his bedroom. But hers was a conventional mind. She tended to steer the conversation toward topics of insurance, doctor's appointments, trips to the grocery store, places in Europe she had visited or would like to visit, and her concern for his unwillingness to return to work (she reminded him that rumors were circulating around the office). Though he knew that it was just her way of showing that she cared about him, he could not help but feel that it was intertwined with her blindness to the wonder that awaited him every night. Perhaps a certain mindset was necessary to unlock the vision. Perhaps there was nothing that could be done and the city was for him and him alone.

The day came when Ben's sick days ran out and he'd have to return to work or face the repercussions of truancy. The night before, contemplating his predicament as he lay facing the foot of the bed, the city was but a feeble distraction. Even the tiny automobiles that now populated the city, choking the streets at traffic signals before, with the green light's permission, creeping forward behind the murky light thrown forward by the headlamps, could not keep his mind from work. If he didn't go back he'd be fired. If he did go back . . . He was not sure what would happen. He didn't imagine that the degree to which he had found his mind distracted would diminish in the least and, before long if not immediately, he would probably be asked to return to Doctor Godfrey. Eventually he came to a decision. Since being unemployed is a form of work for which he wouldn't be paid, the thought of looking for a job seemed even more dreadful than the thought of having one. In the meantime there were bills to be paid. The next day Ben would return to work.

Janeane called to make sure he was up in plenty of time to get ready. His first day back passed without incident and Ben attended to his duties with renewed energy--his time off had been more replenishing than he had imagined. The HR man, from whom Ben expected a visit, did not rear his head. Thoughts of his city, while never vanquished completely from his mind, were not troubling--he was reasonably certain that when it was dark again he'd find it fully intact.

That night, Janeane took Ben out to dinner. She was in a good mood and was extra sweet to him, as if to reward him for returning to his job. After dinner, they went to Ben's apartment and made love. Much to Ben's relief, the city was still there, though something about it troubled him. There was no new expansion he could detect--no increase in traffic nor in animal life in the mountains and foothills. There was something else that he was unable to pinpoint until long after Janeane had fallen asleep. The apparition seemed to glow a little less brightly than it had before, though such a trifling amount of light seemed to be missing that Ben could not be sure.

Things moved on in this direction, pushing Ben ever closer to his job and to Janeane. When his output at work dipped and the HR man reappeared, Ben saw Dr. Godfrey without protest and passed the hours with her talking about the weather or books he had read and movies he had seen. For the time being it kept the company satisfied and he was able to keep his job by completing its minimum requirements.

When Janeane had a falling out with her roommate, Ben did not hesitate in asking her to move in with him. Though his place was not terribly large, it could accommodate two, provided they were lovers rather than friends. Janeane happily accepted the invitation and, after the couple had rid themselves of some redundancies in furniture and appliances, was moved in within a week.

They were a happy couple, though if one in the relationship were allotted a larger portion of this happiness it was undoubtedly Janeane. Ben all the while continued to suffer the slow loss of the city that had once spanned his bedroom. Each night it grew dimmer, if only a little, a fading barely perceptible from one night to the next, but dramatic over the span of two weeks. It was something he couldn't bring himself to talk about with anyone else, not Doctor Godfrey, not Janeane. Most of all Janeane. He would not want her to think that she was somehow responsible for its disappearance, or that he would be tempted to skip out on work again or stop going altogether. It was slipping away, as was Ben's hope that he could somehow again strike the balance that had first brought it into being. He would never see how it ended, never again see the clusters of trees thronged with families of scurrying brown rabbits; it would not remain long enough for Ben to see the emergence of people.

It would go, as all things do. And finally the night came when he opened his bedroom door to utter darkness. There was his bed, his nightstand, his dresser, and all the mundane things that had been there all along, without adornment, without decoration. Was that all it was? He wondered. Decoration? It was more than mere

136

lights on a Christmas tree. It was something he would never attempt to put into words. He knew only that he felt as if he had lost a friend or a beloved pet, something warm and dear. Inside he felt hollow, as if the empty darkness of the room had opened a door in him and let itself in, settling in his legs and ribcage and skull. He wished he could forget it, wish it all away like it had never happened. The memory would be with him, he knew, for quite some time. But he also knew that forgetfulness, in all its mercy, would come as well.

———————————————

Twelve Days of Dragons

by

Mari Ness

Herein. creator... creatures. creation.

1

It was Christmas, and he was fucking alone, except for some polite emails and spam. Huge fucking city, and he was alone. He listened to the sounds of the street, quieter than usual today. Most people had decided to stay hidden inside their houses, maybe to convince themselves that they weren't alone, or maybe to be alone, or maybe because they really weren't alone. He made himself eat, watch TV, check the computer for emails. He ignored the phone. That evening, he looked outside, into the quiet streets, up at the small cold moon above.

Fucking moon.

He watched it for awhile, until he heard something at the door.

Something brushing at his door. He frowned a little, turned his head. It had been nothing, probably. Almost certainly nothing. But what the hell. He walked to the door, opened it, looked up and down the hallway. Nothing, except a small box, wrapped in blue wrapping paper, tied with silver ribbon.

When he unwrapped it, he found a small glass dragon, its head tinged with blue.

So he hadn't quite been forgotten at Christmas after all. He looked at the box. No note; no word. The glass dragon was oddly warm to the touch. He placed it on his table, and then forgot about it.

2

He didn't have to be alone, of course. That was the worst part of it. The woman at the bar three nights ago, who'd been a little desperate, yes, but available. And the girl he'd been talking to online. She'd had things to do in the morning, yes, but she could have joined him in the evening, if he'd asked. He'd had wine, exotic edibles, some leftover crackers and cheese, various chocolates he'd picked up over the holidays, and he could have gotten more. He hadn't asked. He could have called either one today, too. No, he didn't have to be alone.

Not that either of them were why he was alone.

He cleaned the house. Read a book. Did not look at the phone. Checked email a couple of times, sent some meaningless things to a few friends, caught up on blogs, thought about heading out to get groceries. In the end, he sat on the couch, letting the sound of the television roll over him, until that evening, when the brushing sound was at his door again. He looked at the door, looked at the television. What the hell.

The hallway was empty except for another small box, this one wrapped in dark green velvety paper, and a gold ribbon. He picked up the box and carried it to his table, staring at it for awhile. Finally, he pulled the ribbon, and the box fell apart.

Two small glass dragons, heads tinged with green. And--he blinked--one of them seemed to be moving.

Too much holiday spirit. He put the glass dragons on a bookshelf, and fell asleep on the couch.

3

He didn't drink much. Never had. This seemed like the right moment. Some relative somewhere had sent him one of those gift assortments of various liquors, with the clear message of "I have no idea what you'd like, but I'm showing off how much money I can spend on you." He ignored the message and opened the box. Far too many sugary things --raspberry and cherry cordials and the like. Not his sort of thing at all.

A few hours later, his mouth swarming with sweetness, he stared at the three dragons on his bookshelf. It could have been his swarming vision, but something seemed wrong there.

He didn't drink much. Never had. This seemed like the right moment. Some relative somewhere had sent him one of those gift assortments of various liquors, with the clear message of "I have no idea what you'd like, but I'm showing off how much money I can spend on you."

After awhile, he remembered what it was--he'd only put two dragons up on the bookshelf, and yet, all three of them were up there, two of them with necks intertwined, almost looking as if they were huddling together for warmth. Heh. Like dragons, let alone glass dragons, would need warmth.

He needed warmth.

He should call her. No, he shouldn't.

He thought he heard the brushing sound again. Or maybe not; his ears were ringing and his head was pounding, and the TV had somehow or other turned on loudly enough to drown out almost everything except his own thoughts. He couldn't have heard that brushing sound.

He got up and walked to the door anyway.

When he opened it, he felt a rush of cold. But of course. It was the holidays, the cold season. He looked up and down the empty hallway, looking for some sign of whatever it was that might have caused that sound. He saw nothing. He started to shut the door, and saw them: three small boxes wrapped in red wrapping paper with golden ribbon. He picked up the boxes, noting that they had been wrapped with that sort of fake velvety paper, soft to the touch, and they were warm.

Now he was intrigued. Who the hell would do something like this? He scooped the boxes up into his hands and brought them to the table, setting them down. Three warm glowing boxes. He knew what was in them. He thought about opening them. His hands reached out to begin to unwrap --

Stupid. Stupid. People leaving small boxes with small glass dragons was just stupid. He was still alone, life still sucked, and he needed to be drinking a lot more.

He thought he heard something tinkling, the sound of crystal hitting crystal, but he ignored it, and staggered off. Drink. Bathroom. Bed. In more or less that order.

When he looked behind him, the boxes had unfolded, and three small red dragons crouched in the velvety

142

wrapping paper.

Forget it. He simply wasn't drinking enough.

He ignored the tinkling sounds behind him as he staggered off to bed.

4

He could call her. Really call her. It wasn't New Year's yet. He had no plans; knowing her, she probably didn't have plans either. She'd never been much of a New Year's person. He wasn't either.

That night, four glass dragons arrived by his door, wrapped in gold paper and golden ribbon, with tiny golden bells. Unlike the others, these dragons came in many colors, colors that seemed to shift as he moved them under the light. And he thought – he thought – he could hear them humming.

5

He needed to find a fucking job. She'd said so. Others said so. His checking accounts and credit cards were about to say so. A job. Any job. He could start playing again, find a club or coffeehouse somewhere and play a couple evenings a week, maybe more. Record a CD – hell, he could do something himself with the equipment he had, start selling a few, or upload something to one of those websites. Get discovered. Add happiness to the world and all that.

Or even just pour beer. Something.

But later. In a few days. Once January started. Nobody ever looked for a job right before the New Year. It was wrong. And nobody would be hiring anyway, not now. He'd wait for the New Year, spend the next few days figuring it out. He put his guitar into the closet, pulled it out again, put it back in.

The brushing sound came to his door again. He sighed, and thumped over to the door, knowing more or less what he would see. Sure enough, five boxes, in brilliant shimmering purple paper.

Who the hell was sending him dragons?

They couldn't be from her. For one thing, she'd never been that into dragons – she'd read the occasional fantasy novel, watched the occasional fantasy movie, got all hot over that good looking elf in Lord of the Rings, but that was it. No dragon obsession, not that he'd been aware of. Plus, these weren't her sort of dragons. If she had bought dragons, they would have been the fat cutesy ones from Hallmark with the annoying smiles. Not ones like these, delicately shaped, the work of master glassblowers. He bent down to one of the multicolored ones, marveling at the expression caught on its face, coy and withdrawing all at once. And the wise knowing expression on that one, and the clownish expression on the third. And the colors. The glass dragons shimmered in the light, and their colors glowed brightly; these were works of art. Not something she would have bought at all.

So who the hell had sent them?

For a moment, it intrigued him. His fingers itched, the way they did when he wanted, needed, to play something, to send the music out, to get it out of his system. And then he shook his head. Whatever. It didn't matter. It didn't matter at all. Whoever it was would tell him eventually, or not tell him, and that would be it.

He reached out, to stroke the glass body of a nearby dragon. It was still warm to the touch. His fingers twitched. He headed back to the closet, to pull out his guitar, and sat on the couch, and strummed a little. Nothing much, not a full song, hardly more than a couple of chords. But he felt his fingers relax.

On the table, the dragons moved.

6

When he woke in the morning, three of the dragons were sitting on him, their glass legs cool to the touch, their slim glass bodies warm. He picked one up and stared at it, holding it and its outstretched glass wings to the light. He thought--but he could be wrong--that he could almost hear it humming, in little brittle tones, as he stroked it.

Hell, he was just having nightmares,

that's all. He had to get out of the apartment more, that was it. Call a few people and hang out with them.

He steadfastly ignored the phone.

He picked up his guitar and started to play. When the brushing sound came again, he ignored it, playing on. He was somehow not surprised to see more dragons on his bed that night. Six of them, their wings a brilliant sapphire and emerald.

7

New Year's Eve. He should do something, something to celebrate. Go somewhere. The city would have a fireworks show. He could watch that, or get drunk somewhere, or both. Get laid. That hadn't happened in far too long.

He should call her.

When he looked at the phone, seven small dragons had arranged themselves around it, their glass skins gleaming deepest red. He did not need to touch them to know that they would be warm.

8

New Year's. New start. Everything everybody was supposed to do in January. He should do something. Eat something. Take a walk. He looked outside. Too cold to head out and play in a park, but the sky was clear.

He stepped out of his apartment, and spent the morning in a long walk, looking at the barren trees against the clear sky, feeling the city hum around him. He came back to his apartment to find the dragons waiting on his table for him. He moved them back to his bookshelf.

He never opened the door that night. But eight new black glass dragons were on his table anyway, yawning and stretching. He decided to ignore that.

9

She had left him, that was the thing. And since then, everything had been fucking useless. Everything.

10

He needed to leave the apartment, find a job, play some music, dance around, talk to people, buy some food, drink real drinks, laugh out loud, watch some sports. Not play with the nine tiny dragons that had arrived last night, with warm glass bodies and cool glass claws, that had slid over his hands, making tiny glass cuts that had healed almost before he saw them.

He pulled out the guitar again. No need to damage his hands with dragons. He had other methods. As he played, he could almost hear new melodies pushing at him. Almost. He couldn't quite grab them,

That night, ten separate black boxes holding ten tiny glass dragons waited for him. This time, he imagined that they shimmered with different colors

144

that changed as he moved them, placing some on the table, some on the bookshelf, and one in the bathroom. He looked around the apartment helplessly. He had no more space for dragons.

11

In the morning, the dragons had arranged themselves--or been arranged--around his bed. Perhaps he had gotten very, very drunk indeed. They were glass dragons, nothing more. They couldn't have moved anywhere. They certainly hadn't played and danced around his hands, and the only reason his fingers felt like playing today was because, well, he hadn't played, really played, for awhile. Nothing to do with dragons, nothing.

As he thought that, he heard a tinkling sound, almost like--but of course it wasn't--the sound that a glass dragon might make, if it could laugh.

He glowered at the dragons. "Don't think you're inspiring me, because you aren't."

The rest of the dragons had ranged themselves around his living room and kitchen, some intertwined, some defiantly alone.

He picked up his guitar and stared to play. And this time, he knew it was not his imagination when he started hearing the humming of glass as he strummed.

12

The floor was covered with dragons: seventy-eight of them, had he cared to count. He didn't. They danced on the rich ripped wrapping paper; they breathed tiny flames on the boxes; they flew about the apartment, diving and soaring about his head.

His fingers itched to pick up a guitar, and they did.

"I need to work, little dragons," he said.

And for the first time in many many long days, he opened the windows, welcoming the cold and the air, watching and laughing as the dragons shrieked and then laughed, and then launched themselves through the window, flying to the beat of his fingers on the guitar.

———————————————

Green Rushes
by
J.S. Watts

A mirror is a lonely thing. It holds nothing of itself,
But shows the world as others view.
I view myself now. One, two, three, four.
The brush strokes down. There are no tangles left
To tie themselves in Gordian knots.
Hair as straight as a die. As straight as the rushes
Growing green at the end of the garden.

The brush has been here before. Four, three, two, one.
On a previous late autumnal night
I combed my hair in candle light,
Apple core in one hand, brush in the other,
Just to see who came in and somebody did,
Tall and young and as straight as the rushes
Growing greenly at the bottom of my garden.

At other times friends have sat behind me
Reflected in the mirror as they plaited and fussed,
Brushing out my hair. One, two, three, four.
Now it is just one to fuss and pet.
My face stares back at me,
My hand moving up and down with the brush.
One is one, the rushes sigh; two, three, four.

Now there is just me and the hair brush,
Down and down and down again.
I cut my hair the other week.
The brush strokes straight. There are no tangles left.
My face swims down into the depths of the mirror.
I can see the bed behind me, the window behind that,
The rushes growing greenly at the borders of the garden.

146

147

First National Forum on the Position of Minorities in Malaysia

by
Zen Cho

Herein, several voices insight... and some

"Did you see the mak cik?" said Hasnah.

Esther was fiddling with the projector: it wouldn't project. It took a minute for Hasnah's words to filter past her worry. "Mak cik?" She remembered a very old, very small woman in a dazzling baju kurung, wandering along the corridor outside the conference room. "The one with the pink tudung, is it?"

"She's here for the forum!" said Hasnah triumphantly.

"Kidding? I thought she was a guest at the hotel."

"She's the founder of some women's NGO here," said Hasnah. "The Amnesty guy invited her."

"Thank God for the Amnesty guy," said Esther.

The programme timetable meant that they'd only had a week and a half to prepare for the Pahang forum. It had been a nightmarish week and a half for Esther, whose job was to make sure they had enough delegates at the forum,

while avoiding the steely gaze of the mainstream media.

One night last week she'd woken herself up trying to invite delegates in her dreams. She'd lain dazed in her bed and heard a voice talking, and did not at first know it was herself: "... calling from API. API. The Asian Political Institute. No, not Bicycle, Political--yes, we're an NGO. We are organising a forum on the position of minorities in Malaysia. Would your organisation be interested in sending a representative?"

Thank God for the Amnesty guy. Esther had found his contact details in an obscure corner of the Amnesty International website. She hadn't even known the guy before she phoned him up, but he'd dug up everyone with a modicum of civic sensibility in Kuantan.

The result seemed to be a huge number of uncles in batik shirts, but Esther wasn't complaining.

"We were chatting when she registered," said Hasnah. "She told me she's eighty-six years old."

"So old already and still wants to talk about human rights," said Intan. Intan was a long, bony piece of irony, with uncovered short hair and bored eyes. She directed the local branch of a major international non-profit.

"Eh, don't be so ageist," said Hasnah. "Old people also should exercise their right to participate in civil society."

"When I am old I won't care about

this kind of thing anymore," said Intan. "Minority rights ke, religious freedom ke--all that, forget about it. I will be totally burned out. I'll go live in a fishing village in Terengganu and watch the penyu come out of the sea, and I'll never read the news."

"If by then this country is not fixed, then there's really no hope," said Hasnah somberly.

Hasnah was technically Esther's boss, but sometimes she made Esther feel old.

Intan pursed her mouth.

"Still got time," was all she said. "I'm not old yet."

"Ah!" said Esther. They all looked up at the screen.

The first Powerpoint slide said:

First National Forum on the Position of Minorities in Malaysia.

It was in English and Malay. Well, sort of Malay.

"Forum pertama tentang posisi minoriti di Malaysia?" said Intan, outraged. "What idiot did that translation?"

Of course Ming Jun came up just at that moment. Fortunately he was frowning at his Blackberry and didn't hear her. Intan hit him on the arm.

"Eh, you. What is that, hah? You call that Bahasa Melayu?"

Ming Jun flicked his eyes up, still typing. He had the grace to look embarrassed when his eyes slid over the title.

"I couldn't find my kamus dewan that week," he said. "And after that, we already used it for the first few forums, so have to be consistent."

"Next time," said Intan, "go to a bookshop and buy the damn dictionary."

At two o'clock the delegates started filtering into the conference room, greased into contentment by the free buffet lunch. Kuantan wasn't as fun as Melaka had been, with the delights of Jonker Street just down the road, but at least the food at this hotel was decent.

There were forty people today and five facilitators, which meant eight delegates per group--a good number for a roundtable discussion.

"I only have three Malay guys at my table," confided Murni. Esther nodded. She'd only met Murni that morning, when she introduced herself as the press officer of a Muslim feminist group.

"The Muslims don't like us and the feminists also don't like us," she'd told

"I would also like to ask a question. My question is, what is the meaning of 'context'?"

Esther.

"How many feminists?" Esther said now.

Murni laughed.

"Haven't found out yet," she said. "There's one lady from the Women's Society of Kuantan, wearing this sexy baju kebaya. Very tight! I have high hopes for her. Are you rapporteuring for me today?"

Esther shook her head. "I'm with Ming Jun. You know how fast he talks. I'm the fastest typist, so I'm the one who has to have hand pain."

Ming Jun's voice drifted over to them. He was talking to a grumpy-looking Chinese uncle in a green batik shirt. Ming Jun spoke fluent textbook Malay, but he'd studied eight years at the University of Minnesota before coming home, and it showed in his accent. Combined with his ultra-formal diction, the effect was outlandish.

"Sounds like RTM kan," said Murni. "Like the newscaster on the TV."

"Radio Televisyen Minneapolis?" whispered Esther. They both giggled.

"OK, tuan-tuan dan puan-puan," said Hasnah. "Thanks for coming. Just to confirm, yes, we are awarding certificates for attending ...."

Something funny was happening at Esther's table. She couldn't work out what it was.

It had taken a while for the discussion to get off the ground, because the mak cik was at their table. Ming Jun had scarcely finished asking the first question on the list ("How would you define 'minority' in the Malaysian context?") when the old lady's hand shot up.

"Tuan Pengerusi," she said. "Mr. Chairman."

Esther smothered a shout of laughter under a coughing fit. Ming Jun blinked.

"Uh, yes, Datin Zainab?" he said.

"Assalamualaikum and good afternoon," she said to the table. She spoke the beautiful precise Malay of the school teacher: her cadences were a wonderful thing. "Thank you for inviting me to speak today. The chairman has asked a question. I would also like to ask a question. My question is, what is the meaning of 'context'?"

"Told you 'konteks' wasn't Malay," hissed Esther.

But apparently the question was rhetorical.

"When I was an MP near Raub in nineteen sixty-five, what was my context?" said the Datin. "My constituents were simple villagers. We had only one small primary school, no secondary school. The closest secondary school was miles away. I used to wake up at 5:00 am and my driver and I would pick up the bright, ambitious children and drive them to the secondary school

152

in town. After that I went straight to work and I worked until 6:00 pm. Then I went home and cooked dinner for my family and helped my children with their homework. At 10:00 pm I went to bed, but then I would be woken up again. One of the villagers would come: 'Datin, my wife is ill, please can you send her to the doctor.' What was there to do? Who else had a car? I could only get the car out, wake up the driver and go out again. And the next morning, up again at 5:00 am.

"That was my context. To me, it was nothing hard. I didn't think I was suffering. It was my job. Now the politicians say they are very busy, oh, so many important things to do. But if they say they are too busy to help their constituents? I don't believe. It's whether you want to or not. That is what I believe."

Ming Jun's face was a sight to delight the heart of the wicked, but the seven other faces around the table were solemn and attentive. Polite murmurs rose in response.

"That's right."

"True, very true."

Ming Jun cleared his throat.

"Uh, thank you, Datin," he said. "That's a valuable contribution, thank you. But maybe we can focus on the issue of minorities, the definition of what is a minority."

Datin Zainab seemed pleased that he'd brought this up. She said,

"Mr. Chairman, do you know what women are?"

"Um--"

"They are a majority! How many people in this world have a mother?" she said. "How many have a grandmother? All these mothers and grandmothers are women. Yet how are women treated? In my organisation, we support women who need help. The ones who are too poor to buy their children milk. The ones whose husbands beat them. Women are treated like this. They are not a minority, but they are treated so badly. But women have an advantage that true minorities don't have. Women have the advantage of numbers. I believe that if we use our advantage and help each other, women can overcome the way society treats them. That is why I set up my organisation."

"Nowadays it seems to me women are treated better. Men are the ones who are bullied," muttered a man from St. John's Ambulance.

Datin Zainab put on a pair of spectacles that made her eyes enormous. She peered across the table. "What did encik say?"

The St. John's Ambulance man fell quiet.

It was the patience that impressed Esther. They'd had forums with Muslims, Christians, Buddhists and

Hindus sat around the same table. They'd had representatives from every political party going, including ones Esther had never heard of before. They'd had opinionated old judges, belligerent doctors, self-important businessmen, and earnest students bearing downy new moustaches and sociology textbooks.

Consequently they'd had noisy forums. At nearly every one, people had started talking over each other after the first five minutes had passed and they'd forgotten their manners.

But this table was dead quiet while Datin Zainab went on--and how she did go on. As the delegates listened in respectful silence, she told them about the work her organisation did, just stopping short of sketching out their timetable and listing their daily meals. She recounted tales of the joys and tribulations of the women they helped. She discussed what it had been like to be a female MP in the sixties.

"R u getting everything?" Ming Jun texted Esther. "Gr8 stuff! Social history!"

Esther tapped the dictaphone and nodded. Fortunately Datin Zainab spoke slowly, in passionate separate syllables, like a debater. Unlike normal people, she did not speak in fragments, but in whole considered sentences, exquisitely formed.

But when the Datin started to talk about the year she had been lost in the forest and her family had given her up for dead, Ming Jun's conscience seemed to trouble him. He turned to the man sitting next to him, a lawyer with an outspoken blog.

"What is encik's opinion? What do you think the government could do to protect minorities' rights?"

The lawyer had skin the colour of sandalwood, a high-bridged nose, and deep-set eyes hooded by heavy eyelids. He opened his mouth and said in a strong Chinese accent,

"Protect minorities' rights? First thing is to identify who are the minorities. In this country so many people are complaining: I am the one who is bullied, no, I am the one who is suffering. Actually you know who is suffering? It's the invisible minority!"

Esther checked the delegate list. The man was named Abner Ignatius.

The rest of the table also seemed taken aback. But Ming Jun perked up. Sexuality rights hadn't come up in previous forums. People had been too busy arguing about race.

"Correct, correct. That's a very pertinent point," he said. "The minority people cannot see. They are forgotten."

"The invisible minority also needs support," said a representative from Islamic Scholars of Pahang. "Just because our needs are not obvious, it does not mean the government should

154

so easily ignore us."

He also spoke with a Chinese accent. In fact, his voice was exactly the same as Abner Ignatius's.

"Farid?" said the other representative of the Islamic Scholars of Pahang, staring. Farid ignored him.

"Where I live, the electricity supply is terrible," said Farid. "So unreliable! Like everybody else, we also like to listen to the radio. In the forest, the connection is so bad, only one channel is available! Hitz FM. This channel is for the younger people. If you don't like Rihanna, what are you going to do in the evening? Can the government tell me that?"

"And another thing," said Annabella Lim. Annabella ran a breast cancer support group, and spoke in a growly baritone. "The Internet is impossible! Cannot even watch one YouTube video before it dies out. Then you must wait half an hour before it comes back on. Today we are living in a knowledge economy! How is my community going to participate in the economy without internet access?"

Ming Jun and Esther's fascinated eyes moved along the table to Datin Zainab. Her pink-scarved head was drooping. She had fallen asleep.

"But most importantly," said the secretary of the Pahang Consumer Association next to her. He was an elderly man, with fluffy white hair and skin so dark it was almost blue. His voice was the same as everyone else's at the table: a middle-aged Chinese man's voice.

"More important than anything else," he said. "My community does not have any schools. Puan Zainab talks about the school in her village. But we do not even have a primary school. We parents have to educate the children ourselves. The government should consider setting up special schools for our children. SJK (B)."

Datin Zainab stirred.

Esther had gone to a SJK (T), though attending a Tamil-medium primary school for six years hadn't helped her much--her Tamil was still terrible. She knew Chinese schools were SJK (C).

"What does the B stand for?" said Ming Jun.

The Datin had woken up and was looking around wildly.

"Chor Seng?" she said. She blinked, rubbed her eyes and woke up all the way. "Who called me Puan Zainab?"

Ming Jun looked worried. It would never do to offend an ex-MP.

"It's Datin Zainab, not Puan Zainab," he told the consumer association rep.

"Beg your pardon?" said the rep in a pleasant tenor. He didn't sound in the least Chinese.

"It doesn't matter," said Datin Zainab. She was looking--not at the consumer association rep, but at the empty space between him and Ming Jun.

Her gaze was focused, almost as if there were a person there.

"That's what he called me when we first met," she said. To the air, she said, "Chor Seng, I'm a datin now."

The Chinese man's voice said:

"Bunian."

The voice came from no one's mouth. It came out of the air.

"What?" said Ming Jun.

"He said, the B stands for bunian," said the Datin. "You know orang bunian? They are a magical people. They live in the forest but you cannot see them, can hear them only. That is why they are called bunian. From bunyi-- means sound."

"Ah, that makes sense," said Annabella Lim. Her voice was a normal throaty auntie's voice, more English educated than Chinese school. "I was wondering why everybody has the same voice."

Murmurs of agreement from the table. Everyone was looking relieved to have the mystery solved. Ming Jun looked bewildered.

"But orang bunian aren't real!" he said.

"Can tell you are a city boy," said Farid. "If you live near the jungle, you will realise that what is real and what is not real is not always clear. In the forest there is not a big gap between the two."

"Of course, it's all heathenish superstition," said the other Islamic

Scholar.

"Khairul is right," said Farid. "It is all heathenish superstition. People who truly understand religion will not believe in this kind of thing."

"But you seem to believe orang bunian exist," said Ming Jun.

"Ah, it is very hard to have a true understanding of religion," said Farid reflectively.

"We are still working on it," Khairul agreed.

"This is ridiculous," said Ming Jun.

The air snorted. The Chinese man's voice said,

"Oh ya, young man? Then my voice is coming from where, please tell me?"

Ming Jun glared at the delegates as if he thought one of them might be a ventriloquist. Of course, that was more likely than the idea that an orang bunian had actually turned up at their forum.

But the hotel did abut a jungle. Everybody knew what the jungle was like. It was not safe. There were mosquitoes and leeches, which were bad enough; there might be tigers, which were even worse; but worst of all--jungles were full of spirits.

"Why? I am not allowed to attend this forum, am I?" said the bodiless voice. "Aren't orang bunian also a minority? Don't we deserve the chance to fight for our rights? Nobody ever did a survey of our opinions. Nobody wants to know what we think. We are being marginalised!"

"But why are you a Chinese?" said the St. John's Ambulance man.

"What's that? First I'm not allowed to stand up for my community's rights. Suddenly I'm not allowed to be Chinese also?"

"No, my learned friend has raised a very good point," said Farid. "Orang bunian is a Malay folktale."

"We live in the same Malaysia as the rest of you," said the invisible man. "You look around you. Does everybody look the same race to you?"

"I am Chinese also. But I always heard that orang bunian are supposed to be devout Muslims," said Annabella Lim.

"This is what is wrong with our country!" Datin Zainab burst out. "You younger generation do not know how to accept. You don't know how to live together. In my day, whether somebody was Chinese, Malay, Indian, Orang Asal, Sikh, Kristang, anything--we didn't care. When we went to school together and played on the playground, do you think we chose our friends based on race? No. Muthu sat with Ah Ming, Ali played with Jaspreet. There was no division.

"Now people have grown intolerant. They only want to see their own race. The state of the country has become bad, very bad. I remember when I was a child, I used to play in the village with my friend Miriam, she was a Christian,

and I would eat my lunch in her home. Yes! My parents didn't worry that they would serve me food that was not halal. We trusted her family and they trusted us. That was what it was like in the old days."

"That's right," said the lawyer. "Things were better then."

A haze of nostalgia settled over the table.

"I remember when I was young," said the consumer association rep. His eyes went dreamy behind the thick lens of his spectacles. "Us estate kids used to play by the road after school, and the Malay boys would come up from the village on the bullock cart. They used to buy bags of kacang putih from the roadside stall and give them to us to eat."

"You young people don't know what it was like," said the lawyer to Ming Jun and Esther. "You see what we have come to--parading cow heads and attacking churches. In the seventies, our country was so beautiful."

"No, no," said the consumer association rep. "In the fifties, it was more beautiful."

"Looks like you all made a mess of it, then," said Ming Jun distinctly.

This was the American influence in him coming to the surface. Esther winced. Shocked silence reigned over the table.

"How are you humans bringing up

your children?" said the orang bunian's voice. "My child would never talk to his elders like that."

Datin Zainab sat back and put her hand over her eyes.

"You have children?" said Khairul.

"How do you think orang bunian reproduce?" said the voice, with asperity. "I must say, Zainab, humans have become stupider since our time."

"It's the education system," said the Datin. Her eyes were still hidden. "The standards are falling."

This would be like a red flag to a bull. Esther knew she had to speak quickly before anyone got started on the inadequacies of the education system if she wanted an answer to the question that had been bothering her.

"Datin," she said. "How do you and the orang bunian know each other?"

"Eh, I have a name, please," said the irritable spirit. "Tan Chor Seng. But you young ciku must call me uncle lah."

Datin Zainab took her hand away from her face. Esther saw with horror that her eyes were wet.

"We met," she said, "a long, long time ago."

"It was not so long for me, Zainab," said the orang bunian.

"I have changed, I know," said the Datin.

"Not so much," said the voice. For once it was not so grumpy. "Voice is still the same."

158

"Ah, but when it comes to appearance!" said Datin Zainab. "I am a grandmother now. Hair no longer black. Wrinkles, hunched back ...."

"My eyesight was never very good," said the orang bunian. "My hearing only. First time I met you I thought, this woman has the most melodious voice I have ever heard. It is like the stars singing. Now I hear you again, that's still true."

Ming Jun was frowning down at his Blackberry, his fingers flying. Esther was not surprised when her phone buzzed with a text message:

"R they flirting?!"

As the youngest people at the table, Ming Jun and Esther had to keep their speculation electronic. The delegates were older and did not feel the need to be quite so discreet.

"When you say you met," said the consumer association rep to the Datin, "met means dating or what?"

"None of your business," snapped the orang bunian's voice.

"Don't cry, mak cik," said Annabella Lim. She took a pack of tissues out of her handbag and passed them to the Datin. "What is wrong?"

Datin Zainab wiped her eyes.

"I have never told anybody," she said. "I was a young girl then. 35, 36 years old only. I liked to go hiking. My husband didn't like these strenuous activities. He liked staying home and watching TV. But he was always very supportive of my hobbies. We lived near the jungle and I used to go on walks by myself."

"Singing," said Chor Seng's voice. "She used to sing as she walked."

"I wanted to scare off any animals in case they wanted to bother me," the Datin explained.

"All of us orang bunian used to stop to listen when she sang," said Chor Seng. "I was also young in those days. I was impulsive. I heard her singing, but I wanted to know what her speaking voice sounded like. So one day when she was walking past my house I said hello to her."

"That is how it started," said the Datin. She looked down at her hands with their exquisitely manicured nails. "We were very young and foolish. When the child came ... how could I explain that to my family? Chor Seng's family took me in. A whole year I was gone. I told my family I got lost in the forest but I didn't remember anything else. They took me to a bomoh and he told them a spirit enchanted me when I was out walking. He said the year had felt like only a few hours to me."

"Never waste your money on bomoh," Datin Zainab told Esther. "After this, I realised most of them are cheats. He didn't know anything about what happened to me. Guessing only."

"But you were married," said Khairul.

Datin Zainab glared at him.

"And you have never done anything wrong in your life?" she said. "It is for God to judge, not you. I regretted. You think I didn't regret? But I suffered enough for my mistake. After that incident my husband did not let me go walking alone in the forest anymore. We moved when he got a new job, and I never heard my child again."

"You abandoned the baby?" said Farid.

"Encik," said the Datin with exaggerated patience. "If you know how I could have brought up an invisible child, please tell me. I am only a weak woman and I thought it might be difficult when it came to sending him to school. When he raised his hand, the teachers would not be able to see."

"Boon Yi takes after me more," Chor Seng's voice agreed. "His mother not so much."

Datin Zainab folded her hands.

"How is Boon Yi?" she said quietly.

"Doing well," said the orang bunian. "Studies hard. Good at writing but very lazy to do mathematics. I am raising him to be Muslim, like you asked. He goes to my neighbour's house twice a week to mengaji Quran."

"That is good," said Khairul, mollified.

"Nobody asked you, busybody," said the orang bunian's voice. "Boon Yi is very big now, very clever. Can

159

understand a lot of things. He asks about you every day, Zainab. He wants to hear all the stories about you. He wishes he could know his mother."

"I left him my photo," said Datin Zainab. Annabella Lim pressed another tissue into her limp hand.

"Boon Yi is like me. His eyesight is not so good," said the orang bunian. "You know to us sound is more important. He has never heard your voice. That is why I came. His birthday is coming up soon--"

"February twenty-second," said Datin Zainab. "I always buy a birthday cake on that day. When my family asks, I tell them it is to celebrate the fact that even mistakes can have good consequences."

"I want to give him something meaningful for his birthday," said Chor Seng. "I want to give him the sound of your voice. That is why I came. Will you come with me to talk to him?"

"From here?" said Datin Zainab. She laughed a little. "Chor Seng, where you live is so deep in the jungle. How would I get there?"

"Walk," said Chor Seng, as if this was obvious. The table scoffed as one person.

"At her age!" said Annabella. "In this hot sun! Old lady like that, how to walk so far?"

"You are not being practical," said Farid. "You should have planned ahead."

"Orang bunian age more slowly than

160

us," said Datin Zainab. "It is not his fault. But they are right, Chor Seng. My body cannot take it anymore."

There was a silence.

"I forgot that humans work differently," said Chor Seng. "I'm sorry. It is good that I did not tell Boon Yi. He won't be disappointed."

"Ne more of this n Im going 2 cry," texted Ming Jun to Esther.

Esther put her phone down on the table, feeling as depressed as everybody else looked.

Her eyes fell on the dictaphone.

"There is no need to disappoint Boon Yi, uncle," said Esther. "We have a dictaphone here. If Datin records a message inside, Uncle can take it back to play for your son to hear. Come with me and we will do it outside in the corridor. In here it is too noisy. And while we are outside maybe Ming Jun can get on with the discussion. There's only fifteen minutes left, and we only covered five of the questions."

"Shit!"

"We'll record over that part," said Esther.

Outside in the corridor Esther tried to make herself scarce while Datin Zainab recorded her message, but she had to go over to help them find the "stop" button.

While she fiddled with the

dictaphone, a thought occurred to her. Esther said:

"Uncle, if you came to get Datin's voice, why did you say all that about minority rights?"

"Our rights are also at stake," said the orang bunian. "Why not do two things at the same time, eh? Let me tell you, girl. Life and politics is equally important. Cannot separate the two. Both you must take seriously. What I said, you must remember to tell the government, OK?"

"OK," said Esther dubiously. She was going to warn him that going by previous record it didn't seem likely that the government would be interested in invisible minorities' rights, but Datin Zainab started speaking.

"Tell Boon Yi to study hard," said the Datin. "And tell him he must make sure to respect women and treat them with consideration. That is the best way to show respect to his mother. Tell him I always save one piece of the cake for him. Just in case. Tell him--"

"Why don't you come with me and tell him yourself?" said Chor Seng gently. "We are old already, Zainab. We don't have so many obligations anymore. Can't we please ourselves? You used to love the forest, remember? You could come back."

Datin Zainab paused.

"I have grandchildren," she said. "And I have my work with my women. I cannot simply go where I want. And I am old, Chor Seng. My bones like to have soft cushions to lie on. They like to be driven around in a Mercedes. If I'd stayed with you, back then ... but I am too used to my lifestyle now. The jungle, romance--these things are for young people."

"Wrong," said Chor Seng. "Nobody can be too old for romance."

"It is rude to contradict a woman," said Datin Zainab.

"I'm just going to go to the toilet," said Esther "The exit is over there--Uncle knows, right?"

But they were still there when Esther came back. Datin Zainab was standing by the doors at the end of the passage, talking softly. The blinding sunlight outside made a black silhouette of her body. Her arm was stretched out, the hand wrapped around air.

After a while her hand dropped to her side. The murmurs died down. She stood in the doorway for a long time, listening for the goodbye.

Contributors

Luis Beltrán tells the stories of his daydreams through his latest body of digital print photographs. These quietly seductive works hold a deep and moving quality of innocent desire. Figures appear at the ends of alleys, above cityscapes, and up trees; they draw you

towards them, making the eye chase its new companion. Beltrán's photos produce a dreamlike sensation, the product of their deeply saturated, yet muted, coloration. While objects around the periphery of the central image maintain a luscious intensity with their

dark shadows and full mid-tones, the focus shifts as the eyes finds a hazy subconscious perspective. The figures which are central to this misty state call feelingly to the viewer. Beltrán has created a world that captures a sense of the 'other,' and speaks to the mind's natural curiosity. His photos call to a place within us all and echo the inner child's adventurous and courageous nature. Luis Beltrán was born in Spain and still lives there, in Valencia.
www.luisbeltran.es

M. S. Corley is a freelance illustrator and graphic designer who is strongly influenced by literature and the past. He currently lives in Washington with his wife and cat named Dinah.

http://www.mscorley.blogspot.com/
http://www.flickr.com/photos/mscorley/
http://mscorley.deviantart.com/gallery/

An illustrator of the fantastic, Evan Jensen spends a lot of the day drawing at cafes or hunched over his drafting table. He spends the rest of his time doing graphic design and deciding whether to have coffee or tea in the morning.

He has a website of illustrations, a blog of sketches, a twitter stream of nonsense, and other assorted atrocities. He's a member of the SCBWI and helps run Cinnamonopteryx Press.
Blog: http://squirrelsontap.blogspot.com
Website: http://www.fathomlessbox.com
Twitter: @eimhinart

Jaelithe Ingold is a dark fantasy writer living in Pittsburgh, Pennsylvania. She used to prepare fossils for display at the Carnegie Museum and is now a retail manager. Her work has appeared in Shock Totem and Arcane Magazine and is forthcoming in Abyss & Apex.

J.S.Watts was born in London, studied at Oxford and now lives and writes in East Anglia in the U.K. Her poetry, short stories and book reviews appear in a variety of publications in Britain, Canada, Australia and the States including Absent Willow Review, Ascent Aspirations, Midwest Literary Magazine, Polluto, and Visionary Tongue and have

been broadcast on BBC and Local Radio. She is currently Poetry Reviews Editor for Open Wide Magazine and Poetry Editor for Ethereal Tales. Her debut poetry collection, Cats and Other Myths, is published by Lapwing Publications.
For further information please see the writer's website www.jswatts.co.uk and her Facebook page: www.facebook.com/J.S.Watts.page

---

Jeremy Schliewe lives and writes in Tucson, Arizona.

Beth Cato is an associate member of the Science Fiction & Fantasy Writers of America, with work appearing in The Pedestal Magazine, Daily Science Fiction, the MOUNTAIN MAGIC anthology from Woodland Press, and various other publications.
http://www.bethcato.com
http://twitter.com/#!/BethCato

Robert E. Stutts works at a private liberal arts college in South Carolina, where he teaches courses in fairy tales, creative writing, and adolescent literature.
Website: http://www.robertestutts.com

Samantha Kymmell-Harvey is a writer and teacher living in Baltimore. She holds degrees in French Language and French Medieval Literature. Her work can also be found in The Urbanite and Underneath the Juniper Tree.
Be sure to check out her blog:
samanthakymmell-harvey.blogspot.com

Zen Cho is a Malaysian writer living in London. Her short fiction has previously been featured in Strange Horizons, Expanded Horizons, Crossed Genres and the Selangor Times.
Blog: http://qian.dreamwidth.org
Twitter: zenaldehyde

Mari Ness has published fiction and poetry in such places as Clarkesworld, Fantasy Magazine, Ideomancer, and Goblin Fruit, and blogs about children's literature for Tor.com. Her considerably less focused personal blog can be found at marines.livejournal.com, or you can follow her on Twitter at mari_ness. She lives in central Florida, where she is keeping a careful eye out for dragons.

Sandra Odell lives in Washington state with her husband, two teenage sons, two cats, and the voices in her head. She is an avid reader, compulsive writer, and a rabid chocoholic. Her work has appeared in Jim Baen's UNIVERSE, Ideomancer, the anthologies Fear of the Dark and Triangulation: LAST CONTACT, and as audio productions at The Drabblecast and Pseudopod. In her spare time Sandra wishes she had more spare time. She is a Clarion West 2010 graduate.
Learn more about her writing and her taste for the odd at http://sandramodell.com/

Lisa M. Bradley's multifarious poetry appears in Weird Tales, Mothering, Strange Horizons, Cicada, and other publications. For optimum performance, Lisa requires wide open spaces, plenty of sleep, and liberal doses of coffee. Failure to comply with requirements may result in spontaneous combustion.

blog: cafenowhere.livejournal.com
on Twitter: @cafenowhere

Bruce Boston is the author of nearly fifty books and chapbooks, including the novels The Guardener's Tale and Stained Glass Rain. His writing has received the Bram Stoker Award, a Pushcart Prize, the Asimov's Readers Award, and the Grand Master Award of the Science Fiction Poetry Association.

http://www.bruceboston.com/

Julia Rios writes speculative prose and poetry, hosts the Outer Alliance Podcast, And travels a great deal in dreams. She has blue hair and brown eyes, though these things are subject to change without notice.

http://www.juliarios.com, @omgjulia on twitter

Michael Furlong hails from Central Florida. His research interests include film, graphic novels, pulps, horror and speculative fiction. Recent publications include Exrapolation, Albedo One and Dark Discoveries. He can be found sitting in a pumpkin patch every Halloween, quietly humming The Exorcist theme, waiting for The Great Pumpkin.

Find me on Facebook at Michael Furlong!

A quixotic painter, illustrator, sculptor and seamstress; **Kirsty Greenwood** is motivated by ephemeral visual misunderstanding, transient half-light, ocular strangeness, nightmares, dreams and fleeting glimpses of unreality, as well as standard beauty. Inspired by Faerie tales, myths and legends, ailuroanthropy, horror, lycanthropy, nature, Alice-syndrome and transformations, childhood memories, ghost stories, naiveté and true romanticism, her idiosyncratic work often has its roots in dreamlike non-realities which create Art contained by the mind-set of renovating these 'deliberations' or 'visions' into images which often convey the feelings of otherworldly states and her sometimes macabre preoccupations with such.

Alexandra Seidel (Poetry Editor, Interviews, Reviews) Alexa has a powerful affection for the unreal and strange, the weird, the wicked, and naturally, the beautiful. She loves speculative writing because all these things come together there with the power to create universes. She is on board as an interviewer since Issue Two

164

and joined the FU staff as "badass" poetry editor and reviewer soon after. She keeps random thoughts and a bibliography of her own work at her blog:
www.tigerinthematchstickbox.blogspot.com
You can also follow her on Twitter @Alexa_Seidel

(Review queries may be send to Alexa at poetry-editor@fantastique-unfettered.com)

Brandon H. Bell is the author of Elegant Threat, published in the M-Brane Double along with Alex Jeffer's The New People. He is co-editor of The Aether Age: Helios & managing/fiction editor of Fantastique Unfettered: A Periodical of Liberated Literature.

His work has appeared in publications from Hadley Rille and M-Brane SF, as well as zines such as Everyday Weirdness, Nossa Morte, and The Lovecraft Ezine.

He is an advocate for sensible copyright and Creative Commons licensing, a member of the Outer Alliance (supporting his GBLTQ counterparts in the genre community) and a Rissho Kosei-kai Buddhist.
google: +Brandon H. Bell
blog: http://www.nithska.blogspot.com

(/Prolefeed)

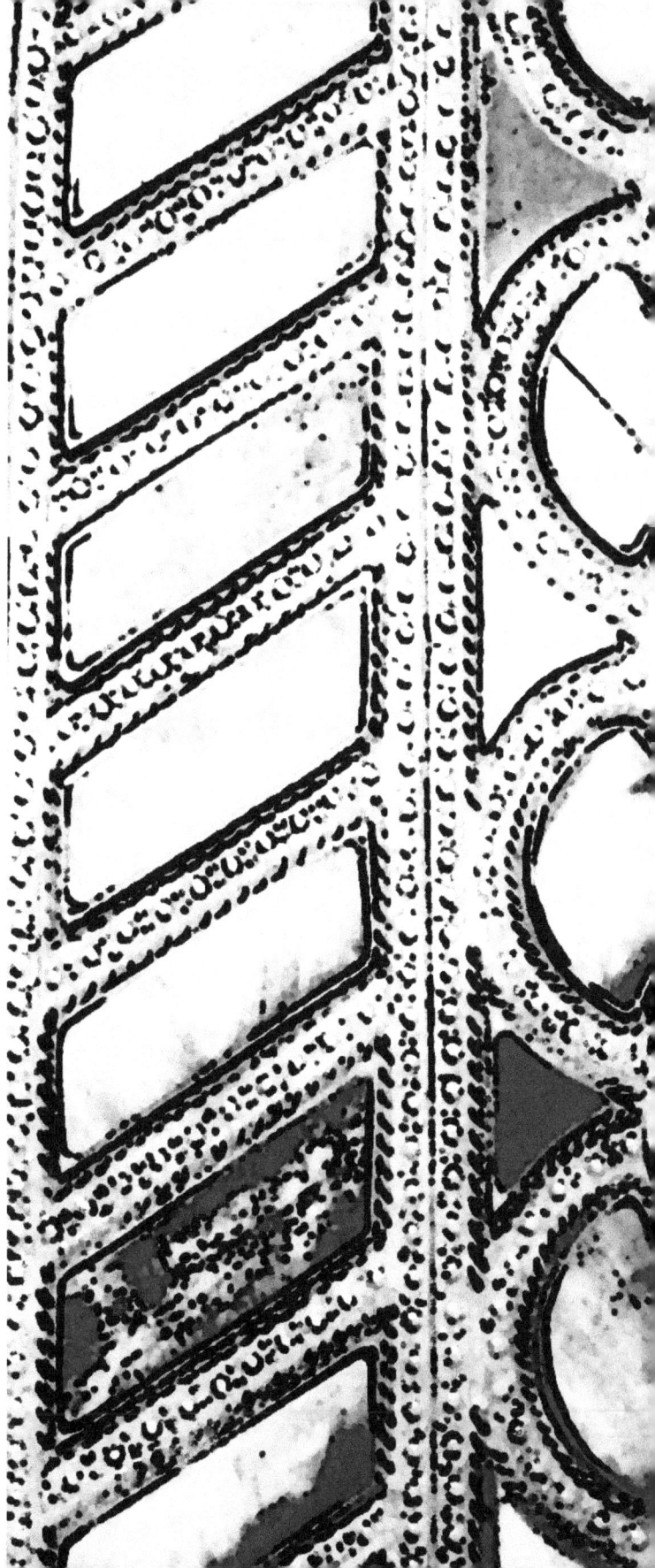

A PERIODICAL OF LIBERATED LITERATURE
FANTASTIQUE UNFETTERED
(KALPA)
PREMIER ISSUE
FEATURING WORKS BY
Bruce Boston
Natania Barron
Rochita Loenen-Ruiz
J. Michael Shell
Mary J. Daley
Frank Ard
and more...
FANTASTIQUE UNFETTERED ISSUE 1 - WINTER 2010
M-BRANE PRESS PUBLICATION

A PERIODICAL OF LIBERATED LITERATURE
FANTASTIQUE UNFETTERED
(UNLESS)
FEATURING WORKS BY
Therese Arkenberg
Lawrence Conquest
Jude-Marie Green
and more...
NEW
AETHER AGE
FICTION!
WHY CREATIVE COMMONS?
FANTASTIQUE UNFETTERED ISSUE 2
M-BRANE PRESS PUBLICATION

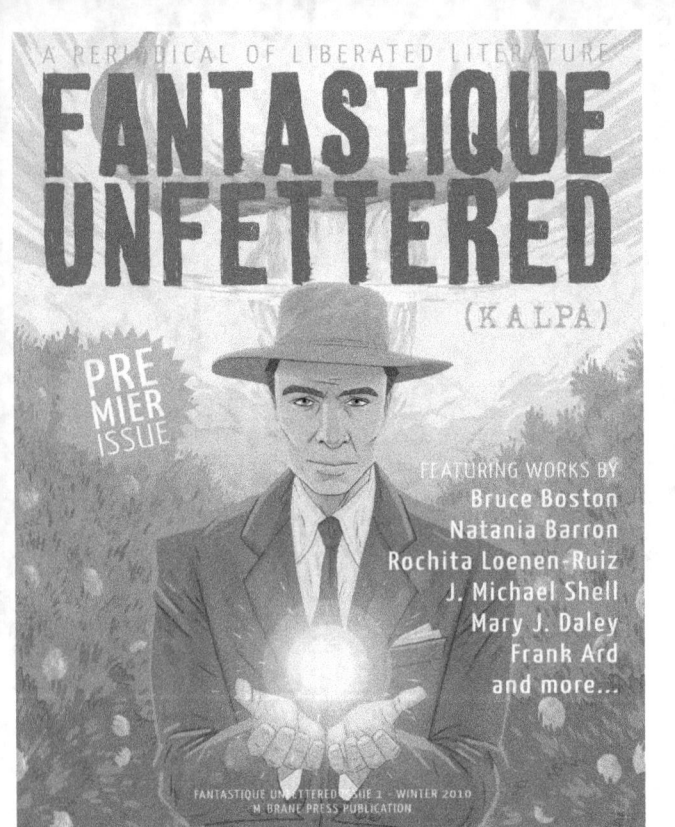

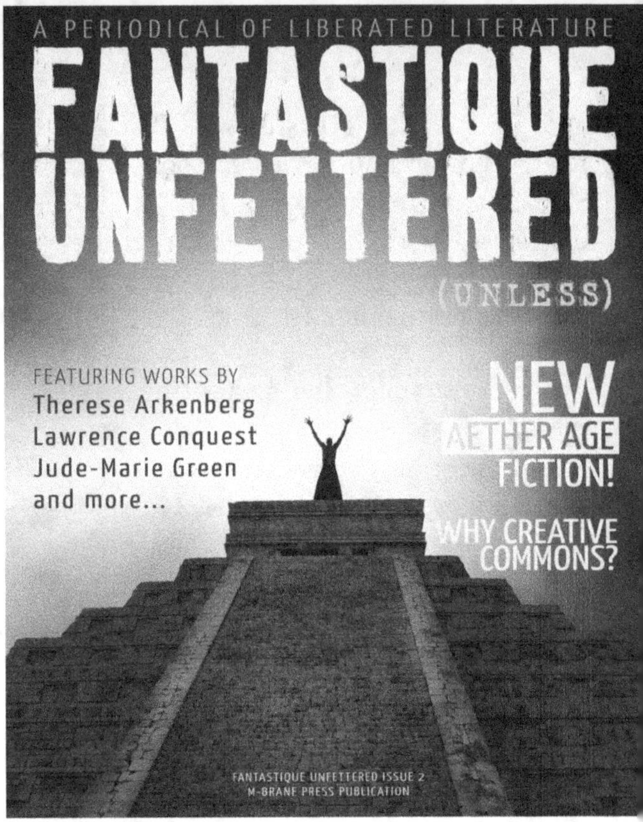

Back issues available via Amazon,
Barnes & Noble, Powell's, and more.

A PERIODICAL OF LIBERATED LITERATURE

FANTASTIQUE UNFETTERED

(RALEWING)

ISSUE 4 COMING DECEMBER 2011

FEATURING HAL DUNCAN'S
SONS OF THE LAW
WITH A
MIKE ALLEN
SPECIAL FEATURE

M-BRANE PRESS PUBLICATION

www.ingramcontent.com/pod-product-compliance
Lightning Source LLC
Chambersburg PA
CBHW082226140626
46556CB00020B/3344